LOVE AND CARNAGE

IN DEATH COMES LOVE

by

Tim Deaton

Contents

Introduction

The civil war has been dragging on for years now, with no end in sight. The body count is mounting on both sides. The number of wounded and maimed is staggering. Whole families are lost and generations decimated. What will it take to end this? These are truly dark times for the country, but somehow, love blossoms in the midst of all this death and carnage.

For the Calloways, the war put brother against brother, leaving a heartbroken mother in tears. For the Barretts, their family served with distinction on and off the battlefield. While James Calloway was away fighting, he was completely unaware that a nurse by the name of Annie Barrett was keeping him in her sights as well as in her heart. Will they ever meet, or will the war end his life before that fateful day?

Before the war came and turned my world inside out, I was just a boy growing up in Georgia. Let me take you back to the beginning.

Chapter 1: James Calloway

My childhood

I was born in 1844 to Eugene and Marina Calloway. I was the third of four children. There was Patrick, Dianna, myself, and William. We grew up on a farm and lived near a fairly large city near the north Georgia mountains. As a child, I was always the prankster and constantly in trouble. When I was around five years old, I wanted to see how big an explosion a three-pound bag of gunpowder would make, so I threw it into the fireplace. The explosion was so big that it blew out the back wall of the house. Thankfully, when my dad built the house, he used thick lumber, so the house stayed standing.

I stood there in absolute shock, and I knew that when the rest of the family got back home, I was in really big trouble. It wasn't uncommon to be alone when my parents and siblings went into town. I had finished my chores—I just got bored and curious. I had just started trying to clean up some of the mess when, over the hill, came the wagon. At that point, I was starting to wish I was dead, and I was convinced that was what was going to happen to me. I looked up, and the wagon had stopped. I could feel my father's anger from where I stood. A couple of minutes later, he came running down the hill, with the rest of the family still in the wagon behind him.

I immediately started crying—not from guilt, but from the dread of what was coming. He looked at the mess and said, with a deadly calm, "How?" My siblings snickered quietly in the wagon. My five-year-old mind scrambled for an answer, but all I could say was, "I don't know what happened." Maybe I could have gotten away with it if Dad hadn't found part of the gunpowder bag. He came back to me and asked again how it happened. This time, I told him the truth. I'd never seen my dad that mad before. He told me he couldn't come up with a punishment big enough for this. So, he got back on the wagon and went to get more lumber to fix the house.

While he repaired the house, my family stayed with my Aunt Beverly, who lived close by. I was stuck with Dad, cleaning up my mess. My punishment finally came. I had to clean the outhouse and burn the waste. I had to empty out the hay from the barn and put it back in every day. I wasn't allowed to go to my favorite watering hole to swim or fish. I had to sit on my bed while the rest of the family played cards or other games. This lasted for six months.

I was also the favorite child in the family. I was born with a small hole in my heart and wasn't allowed to cry much. The others really resented this and were always trying to get me in trouble. Did I mention that I was really pampered? So, my only means of survival was to become viciously creative. On one occasion, Patrick made me mad, and I broke his nose on the bedpost, sending blood everywhere. Another time, I collected fire ants and put them in my sister's bed. She had taken one of my favorite toys and set it on fire, so I responded to fire with fire. That was a glorious victory.

Now, just because I was an absolute terror doesn't mean my siblings didn't respond. I had fallen asleep in the loft of the barn one day. Patrick and Dianna snuck up and threw me off. The fall was only about ten feet but enough to break my arm. That's when I learned to handle pain. They told me that if I told what really happened, they would drown me in the creek—and I believed them. So, out of fear, I said nothing about it at the supper table that night. I eventually told Mom the next day that I had fallen out of the loft and thought I may have broken my arm. When she asked what happened, I saw my siblings standing there, so I told her that a snake had scared me and I fell.

As I grew older, I would often hear Dad and others argue about slavery and other topics. The main issue was that only wealthy landowners owned slaves, and those who didn't—like my family, who believed that owning another human being was an absolute abomination—were being punished. This meant that because we didn't own slaves or even believe in it, my father was offered lower prices at the market for our goods. The landowners often lined the pockets of merchants to purposely pay less to non-slave owners. Let me give you an example. The main place for buying and selling goods was Perkins Trade and Feed. When my dad or other non-slave owners did business with them, they would be given as low as 30¢ per pound, whereas the landowners who owned slaves would get as much as 75¢ per pound for the same quality of products.

It wasn't just that—some of the mercantile businesses would charge us more as well. None of this was fair, and I would hear my dad argue about it all the time, but the only other option was to pack up the entire family and travel to another town to buy and sell goods. The idea of moving west was beginning to gain traction. Unfortunately, that wasn't an option for my family or many others. So, we did what we could with what we were offered.

The whole purpose was to force non-slave owners like us to give in and buy slaves at the courthouse. Dad was always an honorable man and stood his ground no matter how much pressure was placed upon him. Now, there was one store that refused to bow to the pressures of the land barons, and that was Godby and Bench Mercantile. I was always in my father's shadow, so every time he went into town, I would go with him. By this time, I was around twelve years old and wasn't quite old enough to understand everything, but I knew that whatever it was—it wasn't good.

When my father went into town, there was constant talk of secession and rebellion. It was mostly about states' rights, but the constant pressure from the federal government kept drawing deeper lines between the states and the Union. They wanted the South to end the slavery movement altogether. The tension was thick in the air. I knew things were getting out of control when the pastor at our church began talking about rebellion in his sermons.

School was no different, with all of us young boys talking about the glory of war and the honor of battle. We would play war at recess and pretend to kill each other using sticks as rifles and bayonets. Because of my family's stance on slavery, I was bullied a lot, and when it came time to play, I was always the outsider and was picked to play a Northern soldier so they could "kill" me. We had no idea that within a few short years, we would be doing this for real.

Recess at school was becoming more and more violent. Instead of just playing, we were fighting for real. If you were chosen to be a Northern soldier, which I often was, you would be chased and beaten until you became a bloody mess. I often came home with a bloody nose and torn clothes. My mom kept asking why I always came home like that, and I would just tell her that recess got out of hand.

Tensions were running high at home as well. Family discussions would very quickly turn into full-blown arguments between us siblings. My father wanted absolutely nothing to do with the thought of war. My grandfather was in the War of 1812, and the stories terrified my father. Now that it was becoming a real possibility that his children might go off to war, he couldn't bear the thought, and it kept him in a state of depression.

The Scorpion

The older I became, the more I would mess with my friends and siblings. I almost killed my baby brother William. One day, while at my favorite swimming hole, I happened to find a scorpion. After I captured it, I took it home and put it in his boot. I was just expecting it to scare him so I could get a good laugh, but that wasn't the case. When my brother put his boot on, the scorpion stung him several times. Up until that moment, I had never heard such a scream. Within a few minutes, his foot was so swollen that you would think the skin was going to explode at any moment.

After a couple more minutes, William became completely unresponsive. I don't know who was more scared—me or my mom.

She yelled for my dad with a scream that haunts my dreams. He came running into the house and saw William's lifeless body. He scooped him up, put him in the wagon, and took off toward town. My mother and I hopped on horses and followed him.

By the time we got to the doctor's office, he was already attaching leeches to drain the poison and reduce the swelling in William's foot. After about 15 minutes or so, William started to come around, and the doctor said that he was going to be fine. He looked at me and just pointed his finger at me. When my parents heard what the doctor said and saw William pointing, their attention turned toward me.

Now, my pranks would usually get me into trouble, but this time I thought I was going to die. When the doctor said that it was definitely a scorpion sting and the only way it could've gotten in the boot was if someone had put it there, I thought my dad was going to literally kill me. I'd never seen him so mad in my life—his face was blood red. I think that if my mom hadn't grabbed his arm, he would've done it.

You would think that after barely surviving that, I would've learned my lesson. My punishment was a month of cleaning the outhouse and the barn of horse and cow manure, plus doing all of William's chores as well. The job itself wasn't tough, but the awful smell was the worst part. That didn't teach me a thing.

Despite nearly killing my brother, my appetite for mischief remained unshaken.

The Swimming Hole

One day, my sister Dianna was swimming in my swimming spot, and it made me mad. I jumped in on top of her and held her underwater for a minute or so. Then I pulled her out of the water and told her that this was my pond and she wasn't allowed to swim in it. So, I grabbed her clothes and ran off with them. Now, this obviously created a serious problem for her, considering that she always swam without clothes on. I thought that was the funniest thing, and after a few minutes, I gave her clothes back to her.

The next day, I was at my swimming hole cooking some fish that I had caught when I heard something behind me. I thought it was one of my siblings trying to sneak up on me and scare me, but I was wrong. It was a giant black bear! I felt the pee run down my pants and thought I was going to die. It was huge—I'd guess around six or seven hundred pounds. When he stood up, I swear his paws touched the clouds. I knew I couldn't outrun, outswim, or outclimb him. I threw my fish at him to try to appease him, but it didn't work; he wanted me. I truly didn't know what to do, and I was desperately afraid for my life. Then, just as he was about to have me for supper, I heard a gunshot and the bear fell where he stood. Thankfully, my dad had been tracking that bear for several days. It had been eating our chickens and was about to eat me too. My father went and got the wagon, and with help, we got it loaded. We ate really well for a month.

I am now 16 years old, and it's election time across the country. War is seeming more and more inevitable. Southern politicians have said that if Lincoln wins the election, the southern states would start leaving the Union. Well, Lincoln did win, and one by one, the southern states seceded and formed their own Confederacy. Soldiers from all across the country flocked to sign up. While honor and glory filled our thoughts, we believed it would be over very quickly.

WAR

Then came July 21st, 1861: the Battle of Bull Run. When we read about it in the newspaper, we couldn't believe what we were reading. Americans were fighting each other, and people were actually having picnics on the battlefield with their children. After this battle, the entire country—both North and South—knew that this was going to be a long war. The South defeated the Union forces under the command of Union General Irvin McDowell. The paper told of the victory and how people were running for their lives.

The town broke out into celebrations unlike anything I had ever seen. Music, fireworks, and gunfire went late into the night. My dad stood there in horror, and all he could say was, "Oh dear Lord, what have we done?" My parents both begged and pleaded for us to stay home and not get involved, but our heads were swimming with duty and honor. Most of my friends joined up because they didn't want to live with the shame of not being there on that great day.

It's Finally My Turn

As the war escalated and the casualty lists grew longer, I knew I couldn't just sit at home any longer… I was finally able to join in early 1863. The body count on both sides is really mounting up. My brother Patrick left for the war last year. I made my way up north to join the

Union forces. I joined the 963rd Indiana Volunteer Infantry—or as they called themselves, "Lincoln's Devil Dogs"—under the command of Major Singleton. I caught a lot of bullying because I was from the South, but I was used to it. I absolutely loved being a soldier and part of history. My company commander was Captain English, and he was a mean tyrant.

My first true taste of war came at the cornfield. It was a 100-acre farm owned by the Perkins family. A quick skirmish broke out, with both sides suffering minimal casualties. I was scared to my soul, because that was the first time the bullets were coming at me. I went from having my heart full of honor to just wanting to survive. It was hard for me not to just turn and head home like some of the others did. For some reason, I couldn't shake the feeling that I was meant to be here, and that my life would be defined by this somehow.

Chapter 2: Battle Of Sultan's Crossing

We were convinced that the war would be over by Christmas due to several Confederate defeats. We heard of our victory at Gettysburg, and our morale was high—we felt unbeatable. That confidence was crushed when we went up against a very determined enemy at the Battle of Sultan's Crossing in eastern Tennessee, near the North Carolina border. That was my first full engagement. It took place under the hot September sun on the 8th and 9th of September, 1863.

September 8th

The Confederate troops were heavily entrenched, and our mission was to remove them at all costs. Fighting broke out in the early morning hours of September 8th. It began as an artillery duel from both sides. Each cannon shot hit its target with deadly accuracy. Soldiers were literally being blown to pieces. From where I was, I could see the Southern trenches, and with each cannonball that hit its mark, you could see blood and body parts flying everywhere. We got the order to fix bayonets about an hour after the barrage started. We began our attack while the cannons continued to fire. It was quite surreal watching the cannonballs fly over our heads.

The temperature was so hot that soldiers were collapsing before we even got close to our objective. When we got within about 100 feet of their trenches, the cannons stopped, and we began our assault. There weren't as many enemy casualties as we had hoped. We stormed the trenches, and the hand-to-hand combat was vicious as both sides started cutting each other down.

Our first assault was repelled, and we suffered heavy casualties. I think we lost about half of our forces due to the battle and the heat. It was about 100 degrees that day. For a short period, things stayed quiet. I think that assault took the remaining energy out of all of us. The night before, we had double-timed for about 5 miles and quick-stepped another mile or so. Everyone was exhausted. Our captain tried to get us out of the first wave of the attack, but command said they needed us to lead it. That's why we were rushed here.

It didn't stay quiet for long. The Confederate cannons opened up with the utmost violent intentions. They started hitting the trees above our heads, causing limbs to fall on us, creating more casualties. There was nowhere to run and nowhere to hide. A few giant limbs fell across each other, so two others and I hid underneath them. At least it offered some protection from the attack—or so we hoped. Others weren't so lucky. We lost several men in the barrage.

They tried using the same tactic we did, moving their infantry under the protection of the cannons. We knew they were coming, but we were forced to keep our heads down. When the cannons stopped firing, their infantry was already on top of us. The violence of the attack was worse than anything we had encountered before. The sound of a bayonet puncturing human flesh, and the scream that followed, is something you never forget. As it enters the body, it creates a suction, and when it's pulled out, blood sprays everywhere.

We were almost overrun when a small detachment of cavalry showed up and helped repel them. After that assault was pushed back, both sides realized that the heat and the lung-burning sulfur were too much, and everything stayed quiet for the rest of the day. Periodically, you would hear a cannon or rifle go off, but that was it.

We took advantage of the quiet and resupplied ammo and water. I decided to try to get a nap in because I had a feeling it was going to be a very long night. I realized it wasn't going to stay quiet for long, and as soon as night came, all hell would break loose. Right now, it's about sundown, and the heat is still almost unbearable. Soldiers were sitting under trees, panting like dogs. Confederate troops were starting to gather into formations, so we knew the time was near.

Right at dark, the cannons started up again. Both sides were throwing everything they had at each other. The artillery commander had lowered the barrels of the cannons so that our shells would go underneath the Confederate artillery. Once the infantry started moving forward, there would be no protection.

Our cannons tore into them like a hot knife through butter. They started to crawl to make themselves smaller targets, but with each flare, our artillery would adjust. It was an absolute nightmare for the soldiers coming toward us. When they got into rifle range, they stood up and charged. We were cutting them down by the dozens. By this point, our cannons were firing only a couple of feet above our heads, hitting the attacking Confederate troops at chest level.

The artillery commander had the cannoneers switch over to canister shot. That's a canister filled with small metal balls that, when fired, spread out and decimate oncoming infantry. These things are absolutely evil. Because of their light weight and quantity, the chances of dying from them were almost 100%. No matter where you were hit, the carnage was unimaginable.

September 9th

Around 3 a.m. on the morning of September 9th, we received word that we would soon be charging the Confederate positions. We were also told that no quarters would be given. Whether they were wounded or surrendering didn't matter—all were to be killed.

Do or die—the battle ends here. We took off our top coats to keep the buttons from shining and covered our bayonets with cloth to prevent any sound. We quietly left our positions and had to crawl about 200 yards, though it truly felt like 300 miles. We finally reached the forward observer positions. Teams of five were assigned to take out the two positions. Each one had two men in them, so with the element of surprise and our numbers, we quickly overtook them. One of our guys grabbed a giant rock and beat one of the soldiers' heads in—the sound it made sent chills up my spine.

When everyone returned, we lay there for several minutes to make sure we still had the element of surprise. After we were convinced we hadn't been spotted, we proceeded toward the main line of trenches. We could see soldiers moving around and sitting by the campfires, laughing and talking. We were almost seen when one of the

Confederate soldiers went to relieve himself. He was less than ten feet away from one of our guys. When he finished and turned his back, he was quickly jumped and stabbed several times. This whole thing would've been for nothing if he had seen us. None of them realized what was about to happen.

We lined up and, with one volley, took out most of the ones in the trench. We quickly got into the trench, and the hand-to-hand combat was intense. Both sides were throwing anything and everything at each other. Rocks, sticks, bayonets—it didn't matter. To be quite honest, I peed on myself a little. We heard fighting further up. While a few stayed behind to finish off the remaining Confederates, the rest of us moved up to where the fighting was happening.

I jumped a soldier, and we struggled for a few minutes. This guy was throwing me around like a ragdoll, and for a moment I thought I was going to die. After a couple of minutes, two more soldiers came to help, and it took all three of us to kill him. This man was over six feet tall and strong as an ox. When it was all said and done, he lay in a bloody pile of his own intestines. I rolled over and lay there, completely out of breath and exhausted. By this point, several of us had made it up to the command post and hospital area. The commander and his senior staff were taken prisoner, along with the doctors and nurses. All the wounded were executed where they lay, and then everything was set on fire. That was the signal that we had accomplished the mission.

We stayed there for a couple of days, resting and gathering weapons, food, and any supplies we could take. I must admit that even though the weather was absolutely miserable, I enjoyed the fact that I could sleep and have real coffee. It was probably the most delicious thing I ever tasted.

After a few days of rest, we received orders for another heavy march. We were to start making our way toward Kentucky to join forces with General Young's Corps, take time off to rest and recover, and settle down for the winter months. We finally arrived in mid-October. We were bogged down several times due to the storms typical of that time of year.

Chapter 3: Camp at Stephens Valley

After the bloodshed at Sultan's Crossing, we were finally ordered to rest and regroup in what would become one of our longest encampments. When we arrived, we settled into a nice ravine that had a creek running through it and plenty of space to spread out. Unlike the other units that were there, we had this one all to ourselves. This encampment is absolutely huge. Not far from where my tent is, there's a small hill that I can climb and see the whole camp. It looked like tents stretched for miles. It truly was a grand sight to behold.

Our first week here, we got settled in and just rested. Most of us took that time to write home, relax in the tents reading, or play baseball. I had heard about it before but had never played until this week. The food is much better here too. We've been having eggs and sawmill gravy for breakfast and some sort of soup for supper. I've noticed that many of the soldiers are having trouble sleeping—waking up screaming and trying to fight in their sleep. I truly feel horrible for them. Thankfully, I haven't been having nightmares yet.

The New Recruits

A new group of soldiers arrived this morning. Each unit will be given 7–10 of them to train. I know that a few of them will be assigned to us in the end. My first thought was, *"Yeah, they're all going to die in their first battle."* I wasn't too thrilled about this assignment, and neither was anybody else. You give these children a rifle, teach them a few things, and they think they're ready to fight.

I must confess, we did enjoy messing with them and giving them the dirty jobs. There were a few who showed promise, but most couldn't tell their right from their left. Unfortunately, we were given the task of getting them ready to fight by spring, so that's what we'll attempt to do.

Most of the training time was spent teaching them how to march, what different drumbeats meant, and how to stay in formation. We spent a lot of time teaching them how to fight and survive hand-to-hand combat. They were taught the proper way to stab someone with the bayonet, on and off the rifle. They learned how to use the rifle as a bat, how to deflect an attacking soldier, then uppercut to the crotch with the butt of it, and finally beat his head in.

After a few weeks of training, most were adapting quite well to life as soldiers. I'm still convinced most will die early on because their heads are still swimming with words like duty, honor, and the glory of battle.

Desertion

There were two who tried to run away but were quickly caught and brought back to the camp. There was a mock trial where both were convicted of desertion and sentenced to death by hanging. They were immediately marched through the camps on their way to be executed. I can't begin to imagine the anxiety and stress of knowing that you're being marched to your own execution. They were begging and pleading for their lives, but no one was listening. Most of the men, especially the new privates, had never seen a person hanged before.

They were given a chance to say any last words, but all they could do was cry. They were hanged one at a time without a hood to cover their faces. The unit commanders wanted everyone to see what happens to the body when a person is hanged. The first man wiggled like a fish out of water—his eyes popped out of his head, and blood was coming from his eye sockets, mouth, and nose. As the second man watched, he lost control of his bowels, and the scream of absolute horror from him was that of pure terror. While he was being executed, most of the soldiers threw up or simply couldn't watch.

Some of the men complained amongst themselves that hanging them was unfair and that they should have just been kicked out and sent home. But how are you supposed to maintain discipline if you do that? After that, even with the extreme boredom and rations getting low, nobody ever tried again.

My God, It's Cold

The days and nights are now getting colder, and soldiers are starting to really complain about cold-related injuries. So not only are we dealing with a food shortage, the wagons are having serious problems getting winter clothes to us. Theft has become rampant throughout the entire encampment. The punishment is 10 lashes with a leather horse strap if caught, but for some, the risk is worth it. Most people weren't caught, and if they were, it was one person's word against another's.

I and several others would stitch our names in a spot not easily noticed. A friend of mine had his winter coat stolen, and when he found it, the one who committed the act received his lashes. My friend felt bad for him and gave it to him anyway.

We've been here about two months now, and the boredom is driving people crazy. It snowed overnight last night, and everyone is enjoying themselves for the first time in a while and acting like kids again. We were all laughing and having snowball fights. It was truly a Godsend to break the boredom of camp.

I've spent a lot of time playing poker and have become quite good at it. We would bet things like guard or cathole duty, all the way up to clothing items. Most of the time, for the winner, it was just getting out of guard duty or other details.

A cathole is a trench about 10 feet long, a foot wide, and a foot deep where soldiers would go and do their business. When it would start to become full, we would put axle grease in it and light it on fire. To make sure it all got burned, someone would have to shovel it around. Most of the soldiers who had this duty were being punished for minor offenses like being late for roll call or guard duty—just minor things.

As the winter drags on, the worse it's getting. Soldiers are getting frostbite; horses are freezing to death. We would use our bayonets and other sharp objects to take the hide off the horses and use it for blankets and coats. The smell was awful, but it would keep the soldiers who didn't have much winter clothing warm. The meat was cut off and cooked. As sad as it was seeing a horse fall over dead from the cold, we knew that we would be fed for a few days.

Firewood was also scarce, mainly due to the number of soldiers here. So, the camp commander issued an order limiting one fire for every three tents to conserve wood. Some of us took our tents and turned them facing each other, building the fires in the middle to help keep warm. That gave us extra wood, which we hid.

Christmas is coming soon, and there's a level of sadness and depression I've never seen before. This is, for most, their first Christmas away from home, and they're really having a hard time with it. Everyone is dealing with it in their own way. This isn't my first one away from home, but it still hurts. I'm handling it better than some of the others, but I'm still sad and depressed. My thoughts are always dwelling on my family and the smell of warm pie and the sound of my dad's fiddle. I just don't know what it will take to end this war. My sole focus is surviving and returning home.

The Deadly Trilogy

Right now, we're fighting a different type of enemy. Malnutrition, disease, and temperature are taking out more soldiers than we can keep up with. Our ranks are being decimated to the point that rumors are going around about possibly abandoning the camp. An average of 20–30 soldiers a day are dying. Frostbite has taken hundreds off the battlefield, making them unfit for duty. We received a new shipment of uniforms, socks, and blankets, but for some, it's too little too late. The damage has been done. Most of us are keeping handkerchiefs over our faces for hopeful protection against the cold and disease.

The weather has been extremely cold. We've been dealing with snow, freezing rain, and sleet. The roads have become impassable, making it almost impossible to get supplies in. The diseases and frostbite are thinning our lines due to the lack of proper clothes or shelters. Some have built shanties out of their wood rations to stay out of the wind and cold weather.

We keep a daily routine, even in the cold. We march around the camp several times a day to keep the blood flowing. Rifle and firing drills are constant. We typically wake up around 6 a.m., do roll call and exercises, mainly consisting of jumping jacks and stretches. Our mornings are usually filled with drills and marching. After lunch, we do more drills, followed by cleaning up the camp. Depending on the time and the need, we might get in one more drill before supper. For the rest of the day, we clean weapons and do inspections. Then there's one last roll call and exercise before the bugler plays taps around 9 p.m.

It's starting to feel like the days are getting warmer, and the snow is beginning to melt. I hope that we will be leaving this Godforsaken place and getting back into action. The commanders have been very quiet about any possible movements. We all believe something is up because we saw a courier bring a giant pouch to the commander, and shortly after that, all field commanders were called to division headquarters. I'm hoping it's orders for a spring offensive.

Isolation and Depression

I find myself becoming more and more isolated. Sitting here in this camp is driving me absolutely crazy. I'm not sure if it's loneliness, boredom, homesickness, or all of the above. I try not to think too much about home to keep out depression, but I feel like I lose that battle on a daily basis. I am usually by myself or around a couple of friends. I feel that's mentally safer for me. With the high casualty rates, I avoid getting to know the new privates. This way, their loss won't affect me.

For about a week or so now, I've been staying in my tent as much as possible. The few men I've come to know, we've become really close. We haven't been doing much training lately, and that has added to the boredom. I don't like it when we don't train; I use that to keep my mind sharp and off of things. When you have nothing to do and the weather is really cold, thoughts of suicide become a real threat. Three soldiers were found yesterday, dead from suicide—two by hanging and one with his bayonet through his heart.

Now that the weather is warming up, we've noticed that some units are packing up and moving out. As of right now, we haven't received any orders yet, but I expect them any day now. That next afternoon, we were called into formation and told what we'd been waiting to hear: we're moving out.

Just as despair began to take hold, we got the news—we were moving out.

Chapter 4: Battle Of Riverside

"Moving Out"

Captain English told us that we would be leaving in the morning and doing a heavy march for about 20 miles. A heavy march is when you pack up everything you own and take it with you. "Our scouts have reported that a Confederate battalion is pinned down near a river due to the melting of the snow that has caused flooding. Our mission is simple, gentlemen. We are to find, attack, and destroy them. All the more experienced soldiers, keep an eye on the new ones—they're going to be really scared, so make sure that they stay calm. Get as much sleep as you can because you're going to need it. We only have a few days to get there or our chance will be missed and they will escape."

I woke up at around 5 a.m. that next morning. I was just happy that we were finally leaving. The camp was really busy all night. The artillery had left the day before due to the road conditions. We had roll call at 6 a.m., and we were given rations of salted pork, salted beef, coffee, and hardtack. We had to make that last because there would be no cooking during the march. The cooks and the medical staff would be leaving after us. We would be able to march faster than they could move the wagons.

Even with the temperatures being comfortable for a march, soldiers were still falling out and dropping their equipment. As expected, it was mainly the new privates. I was suffering too, but being an experienced soldier, I knew better than to do that. I tried to warn them, but because they didn't want to listen, they will now pay for it. Some ate most of their rations early into the first couple of days of the march, and now they will be really hungry by the time we get to where we are going. I ate very little during the march itself and saved most of mine.

Pinned Down

After the third day of marching, we got pinned down by heavy rains and thunderstorms. The storms were intense and severe. We camped on the side of a hill, and nobody got any sleep. Not only was the rain coming down from the sky, it was also running down the hill. It was absolutely miserable. The good news is that this has also added to the misery of the Confederate soldiers already dealing with their own flooding, so hopefully that will give us more time.

We were pinned down ourselves for a couple of days, waiting on the roads to dry up some. Some of the new soldiers are starting to run out of rations. Like I said earlier, they're going to pay. Our scouts have reported that the situation the Confederates are facing is really bad. "The main roads are completely washed out. Our artillery and cavalry are mired down in the mud and will be completely ineffective during a campaign unless they can get them out. The only way at this moment is a full-scale infantry attack, but without artillery support, it's a lost cause. I'm thinking another 3 or 4 days before they can begin to move out of the area."

Our commander is convinced that the Confederate army has no idea we are this close, or they would have a tighter defense. Major

Singleton wants to attack now and finish them off. Captain English was completely against it without artillery support. The Major trusts the judgment of his leaders, so reluctantly, he agreed and said, "No matter what, in 2 days we attack." We spent those 2 days helping the artillery guys get the cannons set up into position on the other side of the river. Even with all the noise, they didn't even notice that we were there. They must have surely thought that an attack of any kind would be impossible due to the conditions.

The roads are beginning to clear up enough for movement. So, we knew we had to do the attack now while we still had the element of surprise. The brigade divided up into 3 groups: group 1 is positioned on the west side of the encampment covering the road to help prevent an escape, while group 2 is on the east side in an open field just south of them. Their mission is to attack on the southern and eastern sides, while group 3 (my group) will attack from the north, over the hill. The whole mission hinges on one thing: not being discovered while getting everything and everyone into position.

Timing is everything. The cannons will start off the attack, and they will fire for exactly 15 minutes. So, 14 minutes after the first shot, group 2 will begin their assault, and as the last cannonball hits, they'll be at the trenches. Our group will wait another 5 minutes and then come over the hill, hitting them from the north. While all this is going on, group 1 will take half of their force and attack from the west, leaving the other half behind to guard the road. The road to the east is still partially underwater, making escape that way impossible. Our order is: no mercy and no quarter—just complete destruction.

"Let's fight!"

So, at 5 a.m. on April 1st, the cannons opened fire with deadly accuracy. You could hear the screams of pain and panic coming from the camp. Soldiers were running out of their tents and cabins trying to get their uniforms on. We had succeeded in catching them by surprise. They had no idea that a brigade of well-rested infantry was waiting to attack. I reminded some of the newer soldiers to make sure they stay calm and discharge their rifles after every load.

While waiting for our turn to go into battle, Tyler Barrett and I were talking, and he told me that his daughter Annie was on the battlefield as a nurse and that he was afraid for her safety. "James, promise me that if I die here, you will help keep her safe and get her back to her mother. She's the love of my life and the only child we have. We lost four others in childbirth, and the thought of something happening to her—I just can't bear it."

"Tyler, I promise you, but don't think about that right now. We have a battle to win."

Somehow, in the back of his mind, I think he knew that he would die here.

I had my two best friends with me, Michael and Tyler. There's nobody else in this entire army that I trust more than these two men. We sat there nervously and anxiously waiting for the order to attack. Then the Captain gave the order to fix bayonets and get into formation. I took a deep breath and attached my bayonet. The cannons had just stopped and group 2 was now fully engaged. Then it became our turn. The terrain was perfect for an attack—it was a slight downhill slope with plenty of trees to hide behind. I don't understand the thought process of the commanders leaving this unguarded.

Once we got into rifle range, the order to charge was given, and we were on top of them before they even realized we were there. We jumped into their positions and fought hand to hand. It was almost impossible to tell who was who due to the smoke and the tight fighting area. Men were getting stabbed and sliced on both sides. I was just about to get killed when Michael saw a Confederate soldier charging at me. He pushed me out of the way and was stabbed in the arm. With it still stuck in his arm, he took out his wooden knife that he had carved while at camp and stabbed the enemy several times with it. We pulled the bayonet out of his arm, and blood was going everywhere. I knew that if he didn't get it stitched up soon, he would bleed to death. Before we headed to the medical area, he took the bayonet off the dead soldier's rifle and stuck it in his throat.

I quickly got him back to the medical area when a nurse came up to me and asked in a panicked voice, "Have you seen my father?" I knew she was talking about Tyler, so I told her no, I hadn't, and ran back toward the fighting. By the time I got back down there, we had complete control of the forward trenches and began moving deeper into the camp. Parts of group 1 came to help reinforce us, which I was glad to see. The fighting was violent, and soldiers from both sides were covered in blood. The death toll on both sides was mounting quickly, and I saw several of the new recruits dead already. There was no sign of her father or Michael, but I had bigger things to worry about. No matter how many battles I've been in, I still can't get used to all the blood and guts that litter every battlefield.

Death of Tyler

I finally got a look at Tyler. He was a brave and well-accomplished soldier. His style of fighting and his tactics were a sight to behold. He would have his rifle under his right arm, held in place by the shoulder strap, and his bayonet in his left hand. He used the rifle as an extension of his arm to deflect the enemy rifle and then stab them with his bayonet. He took out two soldiers at the same time. I had never seen such insanity. He was actually taking on four at a time. Then one got around him and stabbed him from behind, and another sliced him in the belly. I fired my rifle and killed one of them, and the other was killed a few feet away.

I ran over to him and saw that there was no way he would survive these types of wounds. The stretcher bearers were coming back to gather more wounded, so I called one over. They didn't want to take him because there was no way to save him. I grabbed one by the throat and told him that if they didn't take him, I would kill them both right here, right now. As they were loading him up, I told them to find Annie Barrett—that he was her dad. That was the last time I saw my friend alive.

It's now daylight, and the cannons have started firing again. I was glad to hear them because the Confederates have mounted an offense and are starting to make up some of the lost ground. I couldn't help but worry about Tyler, but I'm sure he will die soon. Now cannons from both sides have opened up, and there really aren't many places to take cover. Most of us fell back into the trenches at the front of the camp. Group 2 has again become fully engaged. By now, all of Group 1 has joined the battle. So, what was left of Group 3 reinforced Group 2 to help eliminate the remaining Confederates. We took a position on the other side of the hill, putting them in a three-way crossfire. As we had hoped, they ran back toward their trench line, thinking they could take up fighting positions. They were completely horrified when they saw our troops in there.

Hand-to-Hand Combat

The first volley took out about 30 of them. They immediately charged at us and jumped into the trenches. The extreme close quarters made fighting very difficult. It didn't take long for the fighting to spill out of the trench. The hand-to-hand was especially brutal this time. When you're convinced that you're about to die, you become extremely violent. Soldiers on both sides were using everything they could get their hands on—rocks, dirt, weapons—it didn't matter.

The fighting has now gone into the afternoon, and both sides are still fighting with the same intensity. The dead and wounded have reduced both sides by about 50% or more. I'm beginning to think that this will go to the very last man. The fighting has been nonstop, and the fatigue is taking its toll. We have them completely surrounded, and at least for the moment, we've stopped our attack.

I, along with about 10 others, was assigned to patrol and take out remaining Confederate troops. Then, out of nowhere, we got ambushed, killing four of the men immediately. We fought back, and within a few minutes, they were all dead, and we had lost six of the 10 men we started with. We went back up to the hill and, for the first time, I broke down and cried.

Where I am, I'm not too far from the medical tents and the field hospital. The scene is one of absolute chaos. There's a mountain of limbs about ten feet high. People are running in all directions. The screams of the wounded getting limbs amputated fill the air. We took a few Confederates prisoner to dig a hole behind the hospital to bury the ones that couldn't be saved. I think the field hospitals are a more traumatic scene than the battlefields themselves. All of a sudden, I heard an ear-piercing scream coming from the hospital. When I turned around, I saw Annie running out of the hospital building screaming, with two nurses following behind her. She made it about 20 feet and fell to her knees. I knew then that my friend, Tyler Barrett, was dead. My first thought was to run down there and comfort her, but I knew that wasn't a possibility. My eyes filled with tears as my heart broke for her.

Cease Fire

It's now late afternoon, and the fighting has been going on for over 12 hours. Both sides are exhausted. Major Singleton is absolutely livid that we've stopped our attack. Captain English told him that our men are exhausted and extremely low on ammunition and water. He agreed to wait till dark but said that we don't stop until they're all dead. We spent that time resupplying our water and ammunition. I broke out some of my remaining rations and sat down to eat. I saw some of the ones who ate all their food early digging through the pouches of the dead to get food. The ones with minor injuries have now rejoined the battalion.

One of the scouts reported that he saw Confederates putting supplies near the riverbank as if they were planning an escape from the battle. The commander believes their plan is to try to escape by boat during the night. The artillery commander, Captain Waters, repositioned his cannons so that they would face upstream, waiting for boats to appear. They weren't going to escape the way General Washington escaped the British when he crossed the Delaware. Several soldiers were sent out to be the forward eyes of the artillery.

Major Singleton, Captain English, and Captain Waters quickly devised a plan of attack. Once the boats started to arrive, we'd let them load up and believe they were getting away. Then the cannons would fire canister shot at the boats to decimate the soldiers on board and hopefully sink the vessels, while at the same time the infantry would launch another assault to draw them back into battle.

Failed Escape

As expected, the boats could be seen coming down the river under the cover of night. We let the first couple of boats tie up to the shore and start loading. As soon as they were loaded, the cannons opened up with canister shot and, because of the close range, were able to destroy the boats. Seeing what was going on, the remaining boats tried to get away, but they were also destroyed. Captain Waters and his men are absolutely incredible at their jobs.

While the artillery was doing its job, we were given the order to attack. It was absolute chaos. The Confederate soldiers knew they would be destroyed and fought with extreme intensity and violence. We fought mainly hand to hand for what seemed like hours. The remainder of Group One occupied their trenches, and what was left of Group Two occupied the hill to cut off that route and keep them away from the hospital and command center. Group Three was tasked with ensuring that all the Confederate soldiers were dead and all our wounded got to the medical area.

The fighting continued into the early morning hours of April 2nd, and we were slowly taking out the remaining pockets of rebels. Many of our soldiers were also killed or wounded due to small ambushes the Confederates were hitting us with. I myself barely escaped a few shots. By midafternoon, it was confirmed that all the remaining Confederates had been eliminated, officially ending the battle.

Rest and Burying the Dead

We stayed a couple of days to rest and recover. Everyone took turns on burial duty. It was truly hard to see people you've known for a long time put into the ground. When I saw Tyler being put into the mass grave, I started to cry and walked away. My thoughts are constantly on Annie and how she's dealing with it. I would see her walking around outside sometimes but couldn't go and check on her. I knew she was in tremendous pain, and I felt helpless. I knew I had to fulfill the promise I made to her dad, but how that would be possible, I didn't know.

It took about three days to bury all the dead. After we recovered and resupplied, we received orders to head to Camp Conway in North Carolina to complete recovery and pick up fresh recruits. I really hate dealing with new recruits. We were ordered to stay there until needed, and hopefully, we'll be back in action very soon. That being said, "soon" becomes a relative term—meaning we could be there a week or several months. My heart aches over losing my closest friend. Though I try to push it aside, I can't stop worrying about Annie. I wish I could check on her, but my pre-march duties kept me busy. Every day, I say a prayer for her.

The loss of my dear friend Tyler has affected me more than I thought it would. I sometimes catch myself thinking—is all this death and destruction actually worth the cost? I don't want to fight anymore. I think about all the men and women who have fought and died, and what would happen if we lost this war. My thoughts are always on home and trying to return to a normal, civilized life—because God knows, there is nothing civilized about war.

Chapter 5: Camp Conway

We arrived at Camp Conway around the middle of April, about a week after we left the battlefield. It's located near the North Carolina and Tennessee borders. The weather was really nice and didn't rain much. I'm glad that this was a much smaller camp than Stephens Valley. There were only a couple more units there with us, which made life easier.

Even with the weight on my heart, I tried to focus on the practical differences of this new camp. This camp is roughly about half a mile square, whereas Stephens Valley was about three times that size. That makes getting around much easier.

After settling in, we quickly adapted to the rhythms of camp life.

Our Day to Day

Our first day was spent getting set up and going over the rules of the camp. The rules are pretty basic: don't be late for roll call, guard duty, or other details. We were assigned our own cooks and medical staff. We're not allowed to visit a different chow line or medical tent because each unit had enough supplies to take care of just that unit, and going to a different one could mean that someone doesn't eat or get medical attention. We had to stay in full uniform at all times when outside of our tents. No saluting the officers unless in formations. Like I said, nothing special.

The day would start at first call around 6 a.m., then first formation was at 7 a.m., followed by breakfast. Our breakfast usually consisted of cornmeal griddle cakes and tea. We would start drills around 8 a.m. and continue until around 11 a.m. Then we would break for dinner. Our dinners usually consisted of boiled potatoes or other vegetables. The meats varied, and we would be served pie for dessert, which also varied depending on the season. Around 1 p.m., we would get back to drills until supper time, which was around 6 p.m. Our supper was up to us since we were issued rations of dried meats and bread. I usually would just eat a piece of salted pork. Then from 7 p.m. till 9 p.m., we would do combat training that consisted of hand-to-hand and firing drills. Our day ended when the bugler played taps, signaling the end of our day. We didn't have a specific time to be asleep, but it was rare to see anyone up past midnight.

Just as we were settling into the camp routine, fresh faces began to show up—new recruits who would soon change the rhythm of our days.

Great, More New Recruits

The first round of raw recruits arrived a few days after we got there. We were told that we were to train them, and then they would be assigned at a later date. Now, I wasn't fond of that idea, but our orders were clear. Just like the ones we received at Stephens Valley, these kids are about half stupid, and just like there, once you give them a rifle and a little bit of training, they think they're ready for combat. I told them that of the 150 that were trained at our last camp, prior to the Battle of Riverside, only 22 are still able to fight. The rest are dead or seriously wounded—and they will be too if they don't pay attention to the training. I believe that I struck the fear of God into some of them, and I truly hope so for their sakes.

We would constantly drill them in the techniques of hand-to-hand combat, more so than rifle drilling. The one thing that I've learned in battle is that most of the fighting will be close-quarters combat. I feel that's where we failed the other group of trainees we were given, and that weighs on my conscience. Michael and I were put in charge of the training of the ones assigned to us. When Captain English told us that, I just looked at him and asked, "What did I do to deserve this punishment?" He just looked at me and said, "I'm sure you'll do something—now get out of my tent." When we started to leave, he called my name and, when I turned around, he gave me a half-smile. That was a major compliment from him.

The mornings were spent doing combat drills focusing on hand-to-hand techniques and how to fight and kill without a weapon. The afternoons were focused on rifle drills and formations. We continually trained them so that when they faced combat, they'd know what to do. There's one thing that we started doing with the new recruits: to teach them how to constantly stay alert, we have them rotate doing guard duty at night, and while they're on duty, Michael and I go around and try to "kill" them. We usually try to sneak up behind them and stab them with a stick. If they spot or catch us, they get out of guard duty the next night. If we catch them, they have to do extra guard duties and cathole duties. Not only does it teach them, it helps us stay alert and trained as well.

Even though we do a lot of training with them, there's still lots of free time. Some of the guys have started playing baseball against the other units. We've come up with friendly bets, like whoever wins 10 games first gets out of guard duties for a week—with those duties covered by the unit that loses the most games. It's a lot of fun to watch, especially because it keeps up the spirit and morale of all the units.

The ones who have been fighting for a long time are sick of all the death and destruction and just want to return home and start living again.

I got a letter from home today, and it read:

"My precious boy, I hope that this finds you well. Your father and I are doing well. One of the cows had a calf and was named Rosie because her cheeks were red when she was born. The family has disowned Patrick for joining the rebel cause, and the rest of the family is really ashamed of him. Life has gotten tough for those of us that are against slavery. Some of the merchants are either charging more or refusing to sell us anything. Thankfully, we have the ability to grow our own food and take care of ourselves. We have heard of people going out west to settle the territory, and your father and I have talked about it. Your father has bought himself a new fiddle, and he makes it sing. I can't wait till you get to hear it. Sometimes, I truly wonder if this damned war will ever end. I see the heartbreak on the faces of the mothers whose sons have been lost. Please always be safe and take care of yourself. Your father and brother send their love. Your loving mother."

Yet even with baseball games and training distractions, a darker cloud loomed over us.

Depression and Suicide

Despite the comforts of home, the reality of war weighs heavily on us all. I can see the weariness on the faces of the soldiers. Their deep and hardened stares will penetrate your soul. The loneliness is consuming at times, and even though you're around lots of people, you can still feel lonely and alone. I share a tent with Michael, and even though we are best friends, we will lay there without saying a word for long periods of time. The depression kicks in pretty quickly, and though I try to keep myself occupied, it can be overwhelming at times. I continually find myself thinking about home and long to be there. I truly don't know how much more I can take. I know it will have to end someday—but when, and at what cost?

My heart is still broken from the loss of my dear friend Tyler, and I cry often. I haven't had a chance to check and make sure that Annie is doing fine, but I'm sure she'll be okay. Even though we haven't met, from what I was told about her, she is a very strong young woman. I feel that some of the ones who've been fighting for a long time are getting tired of it and may desert soon. Nothing has been said, but I can't blame them.

Despite the baseball games, loneliness was inescapable. I thought of suicide more often, haunted by death and the possibility of failing those I trained.

It's now June and the weather is hot. We have soldiers falling out and collapsing from the drills because they won't stop and drink water. The commanders think that the new men are weak and will die or run at the first sign of battle—and to be honest with you, many of us feel the same way. That thought is a scary one, because my life is in the hands of the one next to me, as is his life in mine. But I have no confidence in their abilities. Most of these guys don't look over 15 or 16 years old.

When we had first formation this morning, we were told that we would be leaving soon for a place called Flintlock Valley. We were given one day to make sure we had rations, ammunition, and all our personal belongings ready for a heavy march. We were told that we would be leaving at sunrise. It's only about a one- or two-day march, and we shouldn't have any issues with the weather, except for the heat. We will be joining up with the remains of Colonel Marco's Corps, but will still be under the command of Major Singleton.

I was actually excited to be going back into battle. Judging by the smiles on most of the men's faces, they were too. I packed up everything except for a blanket and slept under the stars. I did notice that the new guys didn't really sleep much. I remember when I had my first taste of combat at Sultan's Crossing, so I truly understand where they're coming from. I went around and tried to get them to relax, but that was to no avail. So, I just patted them on the shoulders and told them to remember what they were taught.

The next morning came, and we began our march. We knew that there were Confederates in the area and that an ambush was always a real threat. We stayed on high alert, and even though we had scouts in the area ahead of us, I stayed vigilant and reminded the new guys to do the same. With every shot fired, we would take cover, and after a while, that became increasingly annoying and frustrating. We received word that our troops had fully engaged the enemy. We double-timed the rest of the way, but we were still a few miles away from the battle. We dropped off any gear that wasn't needed in the support wagons and went as fast as we possibly could toward the battle. Our main objective was to be on the line, ready to fight by dark.

Little did we know, the horrors awaiting us at Flintlock Valley would test us beyond anything before

Chapter 6: Flintlock Valley

We reached Flintlock Valley with heavy hearts and cautious hope—only to be greeted by the horrors of war.

We arrived to the smell of sulfur and death. The smoke from the day's battle was still in the air. The surgeons had been treating the wounded all through the night. The screams of the wounded, getting limbs amputated without any kind of medicine, were thicker than the night air.

As night fell over Flintlock Valley, a grim determination settled over us.

Preparing to Die

We'd been working all evening, getting our defensive positions ready at the northwest corner of the valley. Major Singleton just came over and told Capt. English that we are the far-right flank and our mission is to "hold this position to the last breath of the last man." Pvt. Stephens and I have been moving the bodies of our dead brothers to make room for extra fortifications. I've already made peace with the fact that I may die here, and that has brought peace and comfort to my soul.

There's a calmness in the air tonight, and honestly, it's spooking the hell out of me. I went up to the medical tents to find shoes for Pvt. Stephens and myself that were no longer needed by their former owners. That's when I caught eye contact with a nurse who absolutely took my breath away. She had gorgeous brown hair, maybe about 5'5", and was skinny. Her eyes were an emerald green and made my heart skip a beat. You could see the absolute exhaustion in her eyes, but she still managed to smile. I wanted to go over and say hey, but I was more scared of her than I was of any bullet coming my way. I truly do feel sorry for the doctors and nurses during these battles. I just finished digging through limbs and found two good pairs of boots and several pairs of socks for the two of us.

Let me tell you about my friend Michael Stephens. He's a Georgia native like myself. He's a tall and lanky man with a long beard and a deep Southern accent. One thing that completely surprised me when we met was how strong he is. One time, while we had some time to kill at Camp Conway, we held a friendly strength competition. I saw this lanky, skinny man—who looked like the slightest breeze would blow him away—run at full speed several hundred yards carrying eight 20-pound cannonballs and back, not even out of breath. I was surprised at his strength and stamina.

The next morning, the nightmare began.

Round 1

We had no idea of the carnage that was to come. The artillery barrage started at 5 a.m. Shells were exploding all around us, and we had nowhere to hide. I must admit that I did pee in my pants a little bit. We knew that as soon as the artillery barrage stopped, then all hell would break loose. At daybreak on the 11th, Confederate troops began their assault. It was a sea of gray uniforms, and I swear it looked like the entire Confederate army was there. The noise was absolutely deafening. The bullets were whizzing by, and it was musical—almost like you could dance to it.

One of the new privates we picked up at Conway was a few men down from me and didn't look over 16 or 17 years old. He was assigned to us just before we left camp to come to this hellhole of a place. He was so scared that when he would load his rifle, he would forget to discharge it. Well, after three times, he finally pulled the trigger, and naturally, the barrel exploded. It killed him instantly—and the soldier to his right. There was brain matter, bone, and blood everywhere. Some landed on me. The guy on his left had his jaw, nose, and one eye blown off. As I looked over at what was, a few seconds ago, a living, breathing human being, all I saw now was a headless corpse twitching on the ground. There was no time to reflect—the bodies were mounting up on both sides.

The main road coming into the valley is an ambushing unit's dream. Coming into the valley itself, there are hills on both sides, and the road narrows into a single lane with barely enough room to get a single wagon through the extremely tight corridor. During the night prior, soldiers put down caltrops outside our flank and down the main road leading into the valley, thus rendering cavalry and a full-scale infantry attack completely ineffective. The purpose of these is to make a horse fall. When it steps on one, it punctures the hoof, causing the animal to immediately collapse. That would either seriously injure the rider—or hopefully kill him.

Thanks to the caltrops and the terrain, we easily repelled the first of what would be several attacks. It was terrible. The screaming of the wounded was like something out of a nightmare. I heard soldiers calling out for their mothers. I saw one man carrying his intestines and tripping over the trail of them behind him, yelling, "Momma, help me." Thankfully, someone put him out of his misery. It was very difficult listening to the screams and not being able to do anything about it. I knew trying to help would be absolute suicide. The smoke is blinding, and my eyes are burning so badly that just trying to see is incredibly difficult. The dead Confederate soldiers are being used to help increase our defensive positions. Dead bodies make great bullet stoppers.

Round 2

Then out of nowhere, someone shouts, "Here they come again!" They came out of the smoke like a giant gray wave. Bullets were flying at us like someone had stepped into a bee's nest. Our artillery commander had positioned a couple of cannons on a flat spot, giving them a perfect position to fire at incoming infantry attacks.

This was the first time I'd seen exploding cannonballs. Each projectile would easily kill around ten soldiers. The ones closest to the explosion would be disintegrated, with blood and bone covering the soldiers around them. The ones a little further away would have limbs blown off. I saw one get hit in the chest—his body exploded like a giant firework. The second wave of soldiers was focused on our flank. They stayed just outside our rifle range, making it much harder to hit them. Our rifles are more accurate, better quality, and have greater range. The soldiers in the trench I was in were getting picked off one by one. My heart sank when I saw my best friend, Pvt. Stephens, get hit. I got up from my position and ran about ten yards to where he was lying. His wound wasn't severe enough to take him out of the fight, but it would require stitches. He got grazed by a bullet in the side. I'm thankful he wasn't a few inches to the right, or it would've been a mortal wound. After seeing that he wasn't going to die, I ran back to my position.

Now I know this will sound awful, but I knew I was going to have to take him to the medical tents, and that would—or at least I hoped— give me a chance to see that beautiful nurse again who has consumed my thoughts. I felt bad that my best friend getting shot would allow me to be near her. There was no time to think about that right now, even though it did put a smile on my face.

A few of them got to bayonet range. The hand-to-hand combat was very intense and extremely violent. Bodies were everywhere. In the midst of all the smoke and carnage, it was really hard to tell who was friendly and who was the enemy. We suffered heavy losses, but once again, we repelled the attack. Out of the 47 men able to fight, we had 8 killed and 14 wounded—so we lost about half our men. Even though most would be able to get stitched up and return to the fight.

Medical – Absolute Chaos

I took Michael over to the medical tents. There were three different areas, depending on the severity of the wound. There was a house that had been taken over and served as a field hospital for surgery and recovery. A tent was set up for minor and non-life-threatening injuries. Then there was a third area—a white flag area for both sides. We called it the land of the walking dead. It's a roped-off area where the wounded who had been shot in the head are taken to succumb to their wounds. The further away you were from where the rifle was fired, the slower the bullet became, and sometimes it would lodge in the brain without killing instantly. It was very hard to watch them bounce off trees and each other until they finally fell over dead— especially if it was a friend.

We got to the medical tents, and it was complete chaos. The wounded were lying everywhere. The nurses and the boys—who were originally drummer boys and are now stretcher bearers—were running around everywhere. The screams of the wounded and the ones getting limbs amputated were almost unbearable. It's a sound you never get used to. The worst part is that when the saw hits the bone, it sounds like someone sawing down a tree. The ground was muddy, but not from rain— from blood.

After helping Michael, I found a moment to search for the nurse who had captured my attention earlier.

While the fighting momentarily calmed, a more personal encounter awaited.

They Meet

After I dropped Michael off at the tent to get stitched up, I went looking around for this mysterious nurse. I walked around for a little bit and was about to give up when I heard a soft cry coming from behind the house. I walked back there, and there she was—washing her hands and hair, trying to get all the blood off her. I mustered up the courage to go talk to her. All I could get out was, "Are you okay?"

I startled her, and we both had a laugh. I told her my name was James, and she said she knew—and that her name was Annie.

"Wait a minute, aren't you Tyler's daughter?"

She nodded her head yes.

So, we stood and talked for a moment. I explained to her the conversation that I had with him just before the battle started, and she was surprised. She said, "Dad didn't have many friends because he was really picky, and for him to say that, then he had amazing confidence in you."

The Line Is Collapsing

Then the sound of cannon fire grabbed my attention, and I sprinted back down the hill to my position. When I jumped back into the trench, the soldier next to me explained that the Confederate army had broken through the flank on the other side of the valley and was threatening to penetrate the center. Then, all of a sudden, a bullet hit the man next to me and killed him instantly.

Now understand, I have been in several battles, and this almost made me soil my pants. It seemed like bullets were coming from every direction. The smoke, almost instantly, turned into a dense, sulfuric fog. At this point, all the artillery was focused on keeping the enemy from overtaking the center and completely dividing the line. Now, we knew that at any moment we could be overrun by the enemy. We were completely on our own, and for the first time, I was truly scared. I wasn't scared of dying; I was scared of being captured and not being able to take care of and protect Annie from those monsters, as I had promised Tyler I would.

By this point, we had about ten men who were able to fight. So, I came up with an idea that might save our lives. I took four men with me to do a little bit of recon. Now, I fully understand that this is completely unorthodox in the middle of a battle. My goal was to make us seem bigger than we actually were. We quickly found the positions of the Confederate troops. So, we started firing on them and charged with our bayonets. Now, you would think this was a suicidal mission, and under normal circumstances, that would be true. We caught them by complete surprise and easily overtook them. We quickly made our way back to our positions. I truly believe that action not only saved our lives—it saved the entire line.

It's now late afternoon, and we've been fighting since around 5 a.m. We received word that the southern forces have returned to their camp. So, taking advantage of this, I sent two soldiers to fetch some much-needed ammunition and water. Meanwhile, I went to check on Annie and Michael. He was placed on bed rest to make sure that the wound didn't get infected. Then I went to find my beloved Annie. She was tending to wounded soldiers at the moment, so I went outside to gather up a few flowers to try to brighten her day. When she saw me standing there, her eyes lit up. Still being nervous, I gave her the flowers. She then broke down in tears and started crying.

The Creek and the First Kiss

I immediately thought that I had offended her in some way. She wiped away the tears with her blood-stained hands and told me that her father would give her those types of flowers when she was growing up. She went on to tell me that he was killed a few months ago in battle. She was there when her dad was brought in with a mortal wound. He knew he was going to die, but he wanted to tell his daughter one last time how much he loved her. She was holding his hand when he took his last breath. I told her how deeply sorry I was that she had to watch him die, and that he was truly my best friend. I explained to her that I was also at that battle. She said she knew that and was always checking the medical tents to make sure I wasn't wounded. Honestly, it really surprised me when she said that to me.

We went down by the creek and sat there and talked for a few minutes. For the first time in a long time, I was happy—and I could tell that she was too. By fate, a bug landed in her hair, and when I leaned over to get it out, she leaned over and kissed me. We sat there and kissed for a few minutes, knowing that this might be the only time we'd get to be alone and in peace. We laid back on the grass, and I held her tight in my arms. A few moments later, I heard her snoring. So, I just laid there and held her while she slept. It seems that even in all the devastation and carnage of war, love and peace can still be found.

We were awakened by the sound of cannon fire and screams. We quickly jumped up and ran to our different positions. When I got down to the trenches, I found out that our center line had launched an assault on an exposed area of the Confederate positions. From where I was, I could see the entire assault. They were completely caught off guard and were quickly overrun. From start to finish, it took less than five minutes. We suffered light casualties, but they lost about forty soldiers—killed and wounded.

It's starting to get close to dark now. I heard that the cooks have actually cooked something this evening. It was exciting news, considering that I have been living off hardtack and peanuts for over a week now. It's an extremely hard cracker that a lot of soldiers have broken or even lost teeth eating—but I'm not complaining. It's something to eat.

Sometimes, the only thing that keeps me sane amid all this death and suffering is the memory of Annie and my childhood. I miss the mountains of North Georgia deeply. We lived on a small farm, and during harvest season, all us kids would help gather whatever the land had yielded. My mother and sister handled the housework, while my father, brothers, and I took care of the fields and outdoor chores. Mom canned about half of our produce; the rest, Dad either sold or gave away. He believed slavery was a vile institution and refused to associate with anyone who supported or practiced it.

Chow Time and Annie

I hope everything has settled down for the night. I would love to spend time with my sweet and beautiful Annie. Our supper consists of salted pork, beans, and coffee. I, myself, would often eat peanuts as my main source of food. Not only do they make a great snack, but they also give me energy—and they taste better than that nasty hardtack. Like I've said many times, food is food.

As I stand here waiting for my food, my mind once again goes back to my childhood. My childhood was a hard one, but a good one as well. We would rise early in the morning to the smell of bacon, eggs, and warm bread. Oh, how I miss the smell and taste of real, warm food. If the weather was good, we would be outside playing or fishing. We had lots of woods behind our house, where I spent most of my free time playing too. My favorite fish to eat was trout, and the pond that the dam had created made for great trout fishing. I was very self-sufficient, so when I was up at my fort, I would catch and cook them too. We were taught to be self-sufficient at an early age.

Now, if the weather was bad, we would sit in the house, and Dad would bring out the Bible and read from it, and we would sing and dance to him playing his fiddle. He was such a great player, and the way he could make that thing sound was something of beauty. Mom said several times that that was one of the things that made her fall in love with him.

It finally came my time to get my food. I got a glimpse of my beautiful Annie. She was washing all the tools that the surgeon had used—and the sheets too. When I got up to the line to get my food, I told the cook I needed a second plate for a wounded friend of mine. Since food was so scarce, he argued with me. He gave in when I threatened to rip off his manhood and shove it down his throat and make him eat it. He quickly handed me another plate of food. As I walked away, I just smiled and said, "Now that wasn't so hard, was it?"

When I got up to where she was standing, she saw me, and her face lit up. Now, in the middle of all this death and carnage, stood the prettiest angel I had ever seen. Her smile lit up the sky, and her eyes were prettier than any star in the heavens. For a brief moment, I forgot that I was in a war far from my home. We sat and ate our food and talked and laughed. She said that she didn't know if she would have time to eat tonight, so she thanked me and scarfed it down. She told me that she was extremely scared to talk to me. It really surprised her when I told her the same thing. We didn't have much time together, because we were expecting a full-frontal assault sometime during the night. So, we shared a long kiss and went our separate ways.

The scariest thing on the battlefield is the silence. Now understand, I'm not just talking about people talking—I mean no noises at all. Not a single animal sound could be heard—no squirrels, no birds, absolutely nothing. It truly scares the absolute hell out of me. We took turns trying to sleep so at least half of us would be alert at all times during the night. We finally received our shipment of ammunition and gunpowder. Pvt. Morrison and I went around distributing the supplies to each soldier on the line and making sure that they had water and were drinking it. The tension and anxiety were so thick you could cut it with a knife.

Here They Come…Again

Morrison and I were almost back at our positions when a shot rang out and turned his head into a canoe. I immediately hit the ground as bullets started to whiz around me. I got to an open spot in the line and began to return fire. As luck would have it, I was right in the middle of the main assault. There were so many muzzle flashes that it seemed to light up the night sky. After the second volley, the smoke from the rifles and the cannons was so thick that I couldn't see the person next to me.

Most of the Confederate forces managed to make it to the lines, where we engaged in violent hand-to-hand combat. I took my bayonet off of my rifle and used it as my primary weapon. One of them jumped me, and we fought for what seemed to be an eternity. I eventually overtook him and sliced him in the stomach. His intestines exploded out of his belly as if a cannonball had hit him. No sooner was that over than I had another man on top of me. We fought violently, hitting each other with rocks, dirt, or whatever we could get our hands on. He stabbed me in the leg and was beginning to overtake me. Just as he was about to deliver the death blow, Michael came out of nowhere and stabbed him in the back. All I could say was, "Man, I'm sure glad to see you." He helped me up, and with a smile on his face, just said, "That's two."

Oh, My Goodness, That's Patrick!

Dead bodies and screams of the wounded were everywhere. I ran over to help a fellow soldier who was about to be overtaken, and I stopped dead in my tracks. The enemy soldier he was fighting was my actual blood brother, Patrick. I was in absolute shock, and for a brief moment, I didn't know what to do. Do I come to the aid of my fellow soldier, who could possibly kill my oldest brother, or let him kill my fellow soldier? It felt like time came to an absolute standstill. I had only a couple of moments to figure out who lives and who dies—and could I live with that decision?

I decided to pick up a rock and hit him, knocking him out. Then I jumped on my brother and beat the living crap out of him. My main thought running through my mind was: how could he betray the family like this and join them? By doing so, I saved both lives—a decision I would soon regret. After that, I just rolled over and lay there. I looked over at my brother. His face was covered in blood, but he was alive. With the remaining energy I had, I looked over and said, "I'm sorry, Pat, and I still love you, my brother."

I don't know if it was from the blood loss, pure exhaustion, or both, but I eventually passed out. I woke up in the hospital with my beloved Annie standing over me. I immediately tried to get up, and she pushed me back in the bed. With tears in her eyes, she said, "You're not going anywhere, mister. I can't afford to lose you too." So, when she went to check on another patient, I got up, snuck out of my bed, and left.

The battle was still raging at this late hour. I made my way down to the main road, and a flare showed the horror of the night. Bodies of the dead and wounded from both sides were everywhere. Confederate troops were removing the caltrops from the main road, trying to clear a path for cavalry and infantry to advance on our flank. When I got back to my position, I explained what was happening. A few others and I went and set up sniper positions, and every time a flare would go off, we would shoot at them. This is when I was thankful I grew up in the mountains. It wasn't long before the Southern troops withdrew and everything began to settle down.

Just when I thought I could find solace in Annie's arms, a different kind of battle found me.

The Captain and the Bureaucracy

I was on my way to the medical tents to face the wrath I knew I had incurred from her when a courier approached me. He asked if I was James Calloway. When I said I was, he said to follow him—that the captain needed to see me right away. On the way to the captain's tent, I couldn't understand why he would want to see me at this point in the battle. When I stepped into the tent, I saw why—and I was absolutely livid. Remember that soldier I knocked out earlier to save my brother's life? He reported me to the colonel, who then reported it to the captain. He asked the soldier if it was me, and when he said yes, the captain dismissed everyone and had me at attention.

The captain was a tall, medium-built man whom we feared and respected at the same time. He always had a cigar in his mouth—even in battle. He was a very sharp-dressed man who took pride in his appearance and uniform. I heard one time that he even used a cigar as a weapon. He was on horseback when a Confederate soldier jumped on his horse and tried to grab his pistol. Without hesitation, he took his cigar and jabbed it into the eye of the soldier. When the man fell off, screaming in absolute agony, the captain pulled out his pistol, and after a few seconds, killed him. With his typical attitude, he threw the cigar on top of him and said, "What a waste of a good cigar." He was more upset about the cigar than he was about almost getting killed.

He paced around the tent for what seemed like forever. Every time he would stop and start to speak, he would glare at me and start pacing again. I can honestly say that I was truly terrified. When he finally stopped pacing and looked at me with those eyes that could burn a hole straight through your soul, he said only one sentence: "Do you realize the position that you have put me in?" When I went to open my mouth, he looked up and said, "I don't remember giving you permission to open your mouth, soldier. I want to know why you think that the life of a Confederate soldier is more valuable than the life of a fellow soldier. Do you realize that after he got stitched up, he went straight to the colonel and told him what happened? The major wants your head on a silver platter and the rest of you thrown into prison, and personally, I would gladly do it for him. So now, would you please explain why you did this?" I looked him dead in the eye and said, "He was my real brother, and I would do it again. I don't care who he was fighting. I don't care if it was an officer or a regular foot soldier." I didn't realize how hard he could hit. He broke two of my teeth. He yelled, "Get out of my sight before I shoot you myself—and get that blood up, you're making a mess all over my tent floor."

It wasn't long before the cannons started up again. This time, it was on the left of our position. A few soldiers went to help fill the holes in their line, but I was still trying to remember where I was and dealing with a serious headache from that punch. The fighting was heavy, and as expected, it didn't last too long. The Confederate soldiers were quickly repelled. I think that was more of an attempt to check our numbers and strength than anything else.

Time to Face the Piper

By this time, it was once again approaching daylight, and I don't remember the last time I actually slept. I had to go and see my Annie. As I was walking up to the tents, I was dreading the impending doom that was her temper. I knew she was going to be curious about what happened to my face and ask about my teeth. The whole way, I was thinking about what to tell her. I knew that if I told her the truth, I didn't know how she would react. So, I decided to tell her that I fell and hit my face on a rock. I figured that would work.

When I got up there, she walked up to me and slapped me hard in the face—and then gave me a big hug. She said the slap was for sneaking out of the tent, and the hug was for defending her brother. I gave her a really confused look. She chuckled and said that she knew what happened with the captain.

I was surprised and shocked at the same time. When I asked how she knew, she said he came up there with broken fingers, and somehow, part of a tooth was stuck in his finger. I was expecting another slap or for her to question my loyalties. Instead, she gave me a kiss on the cheek, said she was proud of me, and told me she loved me. My heart skipped a beat, and I told her that I loved her too. Her eyes watered up, and a giant grin came over her face. She was so pretty standing there in her blood-stained dress, with blood on her hands and messy hair. This is a dangerous thing for me. Clearly, I would be distracted and worry about her more than I already do—and distraction on the battlefield usually equals death.

By this time, the sun had come up, and the smell of sulfur and death continued to fill the air. We knew that another attack could happen at any moment. I did find out that my brother was taken prisoner, along with about 100 more soldiers. I'm not sure where he'll be taken, but at least I know that he is alive, and I'll make sure to tell Mom and Dad in my next letter home.

As I sit here waiting for the inevitable attack, homesickness weighs heavily on me. I try not to dwell on it, but with little else to do, my thoughts keep drifting home. What grounds me is the simple comfort of knowing that the same moon I see is the one they see too.

Even in wartime, the letters from home reminded me that another kind of fight was still being waged.

Operation Drumbeat

I got a letter from home the other day but am just now getting to read it. Mom, Dad, and the family are well. My father was one of the founders of an underground anti-slavery movement that has started gaining ground. By doing this and being a part of it, he's putting the lives of everyone in the family at risk, but the family gives him their full support.

The organization is called Operation Drumbeat. It's an underground set of safehouses for escaped slaves. This is really a dangerous thing to be involved in. If discovered, the whole family—including the family pets—would be hanged, the house would be burned to the ground, and the land would be given away. Dad built a small house several hundred yards from ours. My mom keeps it supplied with canned vegetables and blankets.

The whole process is: a day or so prior, someone comes and just says "drumbeat" and moves on. Then someone comes to the door and gives a coded knock and says, "I am a weary traveler listening for the sound of the drumbeat." Then they will be pointed in the direction of the building. If there's any variation of that saying, the person will be shot and killed instantly—no questions asked. Then the escaped slave(s) and the one guiding them stay in the building overnight. As soon as it's light enough, they leave to head to the next house. There is always a change of clothes in there as well, and the clothes they were wearing are burned to throw off the scent so the dogs can't track them.

Dad always had a backup plan for everything he did in case people started asking questions. My brother, who was too young to fight, had some of his toys and other belongings down there. So, if anyone asked, he could take them down there and show them that there was nobody but him. This way, he had everything covered.

They had a very successful crop this year. He grew beans and corn on one half and cotton on the other half of the property. Mom was able to can over 200 pounds of beans and corn. The rest was sold, along with most of the cotton, to keep down suspicions and support the family financially for the year. My mom always canned a massive number of vegetables, so her buying large amounts of canning supplies never raised suspicions.

It didn't take long for news to get out about people helping slaves escape. The local sheriff put out a notice about the punishment for helping: anyone caught would be executed and hanged at the city limits as a warning. Anyone caught withholding information would also be executed. Anyone who turned someone in would be issued $100. That was a lot of money, especially right now. So, immediately, it became a witch hunt.

My father wasn't the only one who spoke out about slavery—there were several others as well—and all were part of the underground. Most of them halted their efforts out of fear of being discovered. That put tremendous pressure on the ones who continued to maintain the line of escape. Suspicions quickly started to grow around my family. My father's fear was that one of the people who had originally helped would turn him and the remaining few in to the authorities. Every time they went into town, people would whisper amongst themselves, creating more fear. So, my father told my brother and me to stay there until all this blew over and everyone calmed down.

Well, that actually turned out to be a smart idea. Some of the townsfolk came to the house and started questioning my father about what, if anything, he knew. He told them all he knew was from what he had been hearing. One of them asked about the new building, saying it was suspicious that it was built around the time of the escaped slaves. He said William wanted a place of his own to hang out in. My father told them they could go down there and check it out if they wanted to.

So, without skipping a beat, when the questions started getting intense, my mother walked in with a fresh-baked peach pie. Now, my mother was well known for her pies, and her tea cakes would melt in your mouth. When that aroma filled the air, all questioning stopped.

My mother was a brilliant woman. She was tough as nails, extremely protective, and would kill you if you messed with her family. She was also a sweet and loving woman, whose family was her life. But understand—she had a temper, and if you made her mad, she would become a monster.

Here They Come

Just as I started to doze off, here came the attack we'd been waiting for. This was an all-or-nothing assault. They came at us with everything they had. Their artillery had exact aim on us, and cannonballs were hitting the trenches. Body parts were flying everywhere, and it sounded like some were hitting the medical area. My heart sank to the pit of my stomach, and I was afraid for my beloved Annie. I didn't have time to think about that at the moment— I had to focus on my own survival. The artillery barrage lasted about ten minutes, but it felt like a lifetime.

I just knew we would be overrun, and I knew I would die here today. Then, as quickly as it started, it stopped. In my head, I had already said my final goodbye to Annie. Then I got tapped on the shoulder and asked if I was Calloway. The man introduced himself as Corp. Rogers and said that he and his company were here to reinforce us and help hold the line.

I truly believe I could've kissed him—his unit was our saving grace. I told him to have his men fill in the gaps and let's make them pay for fighting here. When the line was filled, he informed me that he had snipers with him. He told them to go find a position and make him proud.

Wave after wave came and was repelled. I could tell that frustrations were mounting in the southern infantry because, at the beginning of the battle, the attacks were well organized. Now it's just reckless abandonment. The other flank that had been taken earlier had been retaken. I'm sure that added to their frustration as well.

I was starting to feel a little bit sorry for them. It seems like they're being led to the slaughter like cattle. We still have a job to do. It feels like this is, by far, the most intense fight of the entire battle. The intensity caused some of the newer privates to cower in fear, so we had to punch them out of it. Now, when I say punch, I mean that literally. If they didn't respond to verbal commands, we would punch them in the back of the head to snap them out of it. That kind of behavior would not only jeopardize his life but everyone around him as well.

I'm Shot

Their main objective, it would seem, was to overrun our flank and go after the weakest part of the center. They managed to get to the trenches. As usual, the fighting was brutal and violent. Men were being stabbed and sliced on both sides. Then I felt a burning sensation between my shoulder blades that knocked me to the ground. I immediately knew that I had been shot. I lay there bleeding. Thankfully, the bullet passed through me because I was shot at very close range.

The pain was absolutely torturous. I tried my best not to scream, but I couldn't help it. I tried to pull myself to a safer position, but I couldn't feel my left arm. I lay there for what seemed like hours, and all I could do was watch the fighting going on around me. Due to the loss of blood, I kept passing out. I managed to roll onto my back, and all I saw were gray uniforms. Our line had fallen, and they were pushing further up the line.

At the moment, my thoughts were on my best friend and Corporal Rogers and his men. Were they dead, were they captured—what had happened to them? Then my thoughts turned to my beloved Annie. How is she right now, and does she know that our line has fallen? If I was going to die, I was going to do it on my feet. There was a dead Confederate officer near me. Pushing through the blood loss and the excruciating pain, I managed to load it and start walking up the line. It seemed like I would take two steps forward and fall down. After several attempts, I tried to make my way to the medical tents, but the blood loss was too great. I honestly thought that I was going to die here and not see my beloved Annie anymore. So, as I lay there, in what I believed were my final moments, my thoughts dwelled on that kiss we shared. So, with a smile on my face, I closed my eyes and accepted my fate.

I'm Alive?

I woke up in the hospital with Annie holding my hand. It took me a little while to figure out where I was. All I could get out at first was, "I need to return to the battle." Annie looked at me with eyes I never want to see again and said, "My darling, the battle is over and the

Confederate troops took the trenches." I could see that it was all she could do not to cry as she told me. My heart sank into my stomach as I worried about my best friend. Annie told me that Michael and several others were taken prisoner, along with most of the wounded. The soldiers with the most serious wounds were allowed to stay behind, along with the medical staff.

I was thankful that he was at least alive. Several weeks have gone by, and I have regained some use of my left arm. The best part is that I got to spend every day with my darling Annie. Just being around her is intoxicating. I kept telling Annie and the doctor that I didn't want to be sent home—I wanted to join another unit and fight. That created several arguments between us. I never showed how much pain I was in because the doctor surely wouldn't let me go back, and she would worry about me.

She came to me crying her eyes out. She said, "We're leaving in the morning to go to South Carolina to join Colonel Jones's medical battalion to strengthen them and care for his wounded." The tears in her eyes broke my heart, and I could see that hers was broken too. I knew that I couldn't go with them, so we held each other and cried. She kept saying, "My beloved James, what are we going to do?"

So, we went down to the creek and just talked and held each other and eventually fell asleep. There was no way we were going to spend our last night together separately. As we lay there under the stars, her soft southern accent just drove me wild. I held her in my arms, and she kept waking up crying and saying that she was afraid of losing me because she knew that I was stubborn and really wanted to fight. All I could do was tell her that I would be alright. She made me promise that I would go back home and that she would find me again.

The next morning, we were awakened by one of the other nurses saying, "Annie, you need to get up—we need to get going." We kissed goodbye, and she hopped onto the wagon. That's when I realized that I may never see her again. She jumped off the wagon and ran into my arms, and with one last kiss, she walked back over to the wagon and left. As I watched the wagon roll away, my heart was absolutely broken. I was so afraid that I would never see her again. It was all I could do not to chase after her, but she had her duty and I had mine. I will always keep in my thoughts the time we had together. I just stood there, and for the first time in a long time, I was completely alone on this battlefield—and it gave me the creeps.

Chapter 7: Annie

Childhood

All this time I've gotten to spend with James has been a dream come true for me. Ever since I first saw him at Stephens Valley, I couldn't get him out of my mind. When my father died in my arms at the Battle of Riverside, I truly thought that my world was over, but he comforted me and made me want to become even more devoted to my job as a nurse. I've always loved taking care of people and making sure that they're looked after as well. He's been asking me questions about my family and childhood, so one day I agreed to sit down and tell him.

I was born in 1845 to Tyler and Shannon Barrett, and I was raised just outside of Columbus, Ohio. My father owned a stable and a hotel there in town. So yeah, I lived a comfortable life. Being the only living child, I was spoiled rotten. I know that deep down my father was sad that he didn't have a son to carry on the family name, but that never affected his love for me.

As a child, I was a tomboy. I would climb trees, learned to hunt and shoot from my father, and learned to cook and clean from my mother. On one of our hunting trips, we took along the son of a family friend. We were both around 9 years old at the time, and by then we were both amazing shots with the rifle and pistol. We were climbing up a small hill when Mark slipped and fell. It was only about a 20-foot fall, but he broke a hand and a couple of ribs. Even at that age, I instantly knew what to do. I grabbed two sticks and wrapped his hand so that he couldn't move it. For his ribs, I wrapped more bandage around him tightly to restrict movement, but not so tight as to make him pass out. As my father picked up Mark, he looked over at me and said that he was impressed. Right then, I knew what my calling in life was to be.

My Calling

I started spending time around the doctor's office when I wasn't in school or doing chores. He taught me how to do things like stitching up a wound and treating different types of illnesses. He started letting me do house calls and had me authorized to pick up medicine from the hospital. I just absolutely loved doing that for him, and it gave me a chance to learn the value and satisfaction of earning my own money.

As I grew up, I started noticing and listening to people talk about the possibility of a civil war. I just couldn't fathom the thought of a civil war less than 100 years after becoming our own independent country. A war between the North and the South was truly heartbreaking. As the election of 1860 was fast approaching, everyone was scared and nervous about what would happen if Lincoln won the presidency. Southern politicians had already said that if Lincoln did win the election, they would secede from the Union and form their own Confederacy and their own government. War was now inevitable.

As young men flocked to join the army, their heads were full of glory and honor. Nobody was expecting this to last, and they believed the Confederacy would fold at the first fire of a rifle. Many older men also left their families to join, and that included my father.

My mother and I begged and pleaded for him not to join, but he insisted. He said that it was his duty to defend the Constitution and the country. After my father left, my uncle and his wife moved into one of the rooms at my family's hotel in town so that they could help keep an eye on us and manage the property.

My uncle couldn't join up because, as a teen, he had been shot in the leg, making walking quite difficult for him. With my father now gone, Mom was very sad and would often lie in bed crying and calling out his name. It truly broke my heart for her because she just wanted to stay in bed and be sad. I tried all the time to get her up, but she refused. See, they literally grew up together. Her parents and his parents were best friends, and they spent all their childhood together. They only dated each other growing up, and shared their first everything together, so their bond was unbreakable. This was the longest they had ever been apart. So, it made life hard for us.

Nobody was expecting this to last or for any shots to be fired. July 21, 1861 changed all that for everyone. We learned that a battle had taken place at Bull Run, Virginia. The Confederates easily defeated the Union troops, but the most shocking thing was that families were having picnics on the battlefield.

My conscience and sense of duty kept me awake most nights. I was always close to my Aunt Debby, and I could tell her things that I couldn't or wouldn't tell my own mother. So, after fighting day and night with myself, I went to talk to Aunt Debby about it. I explained to her my sense of guilt about sitting at home while our men were out there fighting and dying, knowing that I could help save some of them. So that evening, Aunt Debby and I sat Mother down and I explained my feelings and that I needed to join and become a nurse and maybe save a life. She immediately jumped up and said, "I absolutely forbid you to go do such a thing. Life is already hard with your father gone, and now you want to abandon me as well!" I tried to explain my feelings and that I wasn't trying to abandon her, but she wouldn't listen. But through the tears, she said, "I knew this day was coming, and you'll do great things."

So, with her blessing, I went down and joined, and at 17 I became a field nurse. It was always a struggle for me because of my age, but I'm not easily pushed around. My dad was a well-known man in the community, which made it easy to find out where he was and to have myself attached to the unit he was with.

After receiving my assignment, the journey from eager student to field nurse became real.

My First Assignment

I finally arrived at their camp at Stephens Valley. I immediately went to find my father. I missed him so much and couldn't wait to finally see him. When he first saw me, he was happy and angry at the same time. He said in a worried voice, "This is no place for you. What are you doing here?" I politely told him, "This is the calling that God placed on my life, and if you have a problem with me being here, well, then just take it up with God because I'm not leaving!" He smiled and said to me, "I didn't raise a weak woman, and I feel sorry for whoever gets in your way." I assured him that Uncle Larry and Aunt Debby were helping Mother and taking care of everything. All he needed to do was stay focused, survive, and come home.

When I first got to camp, I didn't get to see much of my father at all. My days were filled with duties that a housewife would perform—getting food and water for the male doctors and nurses, cleaning, and anything that was non-medical. I was constantly bullied by the other nurses because I was so young, but that didn't discourage me. In fact, it made my resolve that much stronger. Since I was half the age of the other nurses, they refused to teach me anything and would often tell me to go back home and play with my dolls. That really made me angry, but I would never let them see it.

I didn't know what was worse—the sexual advances from the doctors or the continual bullying from the nurses. The doctors would walk by and slap me on the bottom really hard or squeeze it. They would try to pull up my dress when I was bent over grabbing something, and they would make comments about how they would love to play with my breasts. The nurses weren't much better. They would purposely trip me and make me fall. I ate alone because nobody would talk to me. They would walk by and grab my food, throw it on the ground, and step on it. Through all of that, they never saw me cry or lash out at them, even though inside I was very angry. My sense of duty outweighed all the harassment that I faced daily. I never told my father about any of the things that happened to me. I needed him to focus on his survival, not worry about my safety.

As the winter progressed and the temperatures continued to fall, I found that most of my time was spent treating frostbite and helping ease the suffering of those who had gotten sick or were now suffering from dysentery and other diseases. Since most of the nurses' four-month tour of duty was coming to an end, I really felt cheated because I hadn't been taught much. Most of them left because they hadn't received any pay for a couple of months. So, I contacted Doctor Shaw back home to send me any and all information he had about the diseases that were plaguing the camp. About three weeks later, a trunk arrived for me filled with books, medicine, and a note that simply said, "You've made me very proud of you, Nurse Annie. I can't wait till you come home. I want to hire you as my full-time nurse and medical assistant." I screamed with excitement.

The fact that over half of the nurses left the camp and headed home really worked in my favor. See, now the doctors were forced to treat me better and teach me. They quickly learned that I wasn't just some stupid teenager, but an intelligent and very competent nurse.

My Daily Routine

My routine was very structured, and the days were long. I was usually up by 4 a.m., and got myself ready for the day ahead by 5 a.m. I rarely ate breakfast, but I drank plenty of coffee. I just wanted to get to helping the sick and injured. I would spend the morning tending to patients and helping treat or amputate frostbitten toes and fingers.

When I was done with that, I would clean the tools and make up beds. I would stop for lunch for an hour and read one of the books that Doctor Shaw sent me. My lunch usually consisted of a piece of salted pork or beef, cornbread, and coffee, and, when available, donuts.

After lunch, I would spend a few hours going throughout the camp checking on soldiers whom I knew were sick. I was really surprised by how much respect the soldiers showed me. Yeah, there were a few that made me nervous, but my dad had already talked to the company commanders about me, and I was told that if any soldier tried to harm me, I should go straight to the commanding officer, and they would handle it.

I would do that until around suppertime. My supper was usually some sort of hot soup and a cup of coffee. I didn't want to eat too much because I felt guilty trying to get more than my fair share. Then after supper, I would help soldiers write letters home, read them, or just sit with them and talk. I would go to my "room" around 9 at night and lie there reading until I fell asleep. Then I'd get up and do it all over again.

My room was just a cot and a couple of blankets, a lamp, and a bedpan I would use to put in embers from one of the soldiers' fires, and that kept me warm enough. It was about 10 feet wide and about 15 feet long. These were rooms built just behind the field hospital for the nurses. Since they were quickly built, the wind would often blow through them. I didn't mind it too much; I was used to the cold. We also had our own private outhouses built just for the nurses to use. So overall, there really wasn't much to complain about.

Still, amidst the structure and routine, something unexpected changed everything.

My Heart Skipped a Beat

I was out and about one day, going to check on my dad, and that's when I saw you. When I first looked at you, my heart melted. In front of me stood a 6-foot-tall man with curly brown hair and a short beard. My heart stopped when I looked into those brown eyes. You and my dad were talking, so I hid until you walked away. I had never been so nervous just being in someone's presence before.

I spent some time with Dad, and we talked, shared some salted pork, and some coffee. He kept looking at me and seeing a big grin on my face. He wanted to ask but didn't. I couldn't resist any longer and asked him who that man was he was talking to. He smiled and said, "That is James. Do you want me to go get him and introduce the two of you?" My face turned red, and I got up and walked away in embarrassment. I looked back, and he was laughing at me. My father was actually laughing at me.

From that moment forward, I kept an eye on you from a distance. I really wanted to come and talk to you, but I was truly afraid to. Also, I didn't want to be a distraction to you. I hadn't even said a single word to you, and you didn't even know I existed, but I was in love with you from the moment I first saw you. I would find ways to go and see if I could just get a glimpse of you and what you were doing. I would often go around and pretend to be checking on the soldiers, but I loved watching you train the new ones and how you truly wanted them to survive this terrible war.

By this point, my days were filled going tent to tent with the doctors, checking on the soldiers to make sure they were still alive. Men were dying daily by the dozens, mainly from diseases. The number of soldiers dying from suicide and infections was really on the rise. We just didn't have enough medications to take care of everyone properly.

The weather had been warming up, and the snow was completely gone. I'm truly thankful that we survived the winter. Several units had packed up and started moving out of camp. This was good news because that meant we would be moving soon as well—and that meant fewer people to take care of. I put in a request to be assigned to the unit that you and my father were in, and when the commander agreed, I was very happy to tell my dad that I would be traveling with them. He insisted that I go home, but, like I've already said—and you know this by now—he raised a stubborn woman.

Some of the support units, like the engineers and other non-vital units, had already been moving out. They usually moved out a couple of days before the main units so they could make sure the roads and such were made passable. I had been hearing rumors that a battalion of Confederates was trapped in a valley not too far from here. When I heard that it was true, I went to find my father and give him a big hug. I wish I had known that it was the last time I would get to hug him.

We followed well behind all of you for our safety and to keep the roads from getting too clogged up. Movement was absolutely horrible for us. Our wagons kept getting mired in the mud. It felt like we were only moving about 100 yards an hour. I was really worried and concerned that the noises from our horses would give away our positions and endanger the lives of our soldiers.

But before we could even engage in battle, nature itself became our enemy.

The Road to Hell

We have been pinned down by heavy thunderstorms. The entire unit has come to a complete stop. We were stopped for a couple of days before we could even think about moving again. I, along with a couple of other nurses, covered the holes in the front and back of our wagon so we could stay dry. The worst part was having to get out to go to the bathroom. We kept pots in the wagon with us to pee in, but anything else required us to go outside. It was absolutely miserable—not just because of the weather but also the risk of snakes and other animals.

Whenever possible, everyone stayed hunkered down in their individual wagons, and there was very little activity. We were issued rubber ponchos to help keep us dry when we did have to go outside. I mainly used mine as a blanket. The nights were still a little bit too cold for me, so I slept on some wooden crates with a couple of blankets and that poncho on top, and it was a good sleep.

It rained really hard for a couple of days, so after the rain finally stopped, we were told that we would be moving again in a couple of days. When we were finally able to move, we rode about a two-day journey, or about 25 miles or so. This put us about a mile or so from where the troops were gathering. That's where, for now, we would set up camp and wait for the combat troops to get set up—and then we would move up.

There was an abandoned house about a half-mile or so away from the location of the Confederate troops. I was scared the whole time that we would be discovered and taken prisoner by them.

As the main attack units were getting into formation, I saw you and my father but wasn't able to get up to where you were. The head nurse came up to me and told me to go try to take a nap, because once this starts, we're going to get really busy really quick. I was sleeping really well in the back of the wagon when the cannons started. I almost jumped out of my skin. I saw your unit walk up to the top and over the hill. It was an amazing sight to see. I knew what was coming after the cannons stopped.

Battle of Riverside

I could hear the screams and the noise of the rifles. It wasn't too long before the wounded started pouring in to us. It was hard for me to stay focused because I knew that you and my father were in the middle of the fighting. I had to put that out of my head to focus on the job at hand. Everyone that was brought in—I had to make eye contact to make sure that it wasn't either of you. It has been nonstop for—I don't know—for what seems like hours, and the wounded just keep pouring into the medical areas.

When I saw you come over the hill carrying a wounded soldier, my heart stopped beating. I was so afraid that it was you bringing my father, but I was relieved when I saw that it wasn't him.

"No, Daddy, no!"

Shortly after, one of the nurses came running up to me with tears in her eyes and said, "They just brought your father in and it's really bad. You better go—I'll take over here." I ran over to where he was, and when I saw him lying there, covered in his blood and with parts of his intestines hanging out, I immediately started crying uncontrollably. I knew that this type of wound would mean his death. I regained some of my composure and walked over and grabbed his hand. He looked up at me and, with a soft, gentle voice, said, "My precious dear Annie, I love you so much, and I needed to tell you how proud I am of you and what you've accomplished so far in your life."

"Daddy, please don't die. You're going to survive this, and I love you too."

"Annie, I…"

I watched him take his last breath. I ran out of the tent screaming as loud as I could. I made it a few feet before collapsing. My world had just come to an end. Some of the nurses brought me back inside and gave me a shot of morphine to put me to sleep. They knew that I was going to be no help to anyone after that. By the time I woke up, I was in the back of a wagon and the battle was over. I lay there for what seemed like days, crying and thinking about how I was going to tell Mother about his death. I knew that this would be the end of her.

Amid this despair, a new friendship began to blossom.

We had so many wounded still that weren't able to be transported to a field hospital, so I knew I had time here before moving on. I wrote a letter to Aunt Debby telling her about the death of her brother but still had no idea how to tell Mom. I thought about just waiting till I got home from the war, but that wasn't a possibility, and I knew that she would hate me for it. So, I wrote and told Mom about it. I told her how brave of a soldier he was and that he died valiantly and with honor. I made sure that she was aware that I was there for him when he took his last breath.

About a week or two later, I got a letter from my aunt wanting me to come home. She said that Mom had stopped eating and refused to drink anything. She said that Shannon had said many times that her life was over and that she needed to die so she could go be with her beloved Tyler. I didn't know what to do. I needed to go home to try to take care of Mother, but that would take easily a week or so to get there.

Lizzy

Over the past month or so, I became friends with a new nurse by the name of Elizabeth, or Lizzy for short. She was kind and never harassed me because of my young age. Actually, she got most of the bullying stopped, and I was grateful. She was about 35 years old, with brown hair and green eyes. She came in from northern Indiana to help fill the nurse shortage. She would always tell jokes to the wounded soldiers to try to cheer them up. She was truly a gentle soul.

One day, she saw me sitting under a tree crying and came over to ask me if I thought I had watered that tree enough, or if I was going to keep trying. I smiled, and she sat down beside me and let me cry on her shoulder. It feels like I cried for an hour. I told her about Mom and how I was torn between duty and family, and how I was afraid that I might not make it home to Ohio in time to save her.

She looked at me with tears in her eyes and said, "Baby, you have to follow your heart. You are truly a very intelligent and beautiful woman, and brave enough to do what you feel is right."

I went back inside and, while standing in the doorway, looked at the wounded lying in the beds, suffering. So, with a very heavy heart, I decided to stay.

Heading to Camp Conway

A couple of weeks have passed, and now it was time to move on to join another unit. My thoughts were always on you, and I was so scared I would never see you again. We traveled to a field hospital to pick up medical supplies and then headed toward Camp Conway. All I knew was that it was a smaller camp and that only a couple of units would be there.

While at the field hospital, I spent most of my time helping treat the wounded and learned some new medical procedures that I feel will really increase their chances of survival. We learned that using certain plants carried antiseptic properties and would help keep gangrene from forming in the wounds of amputees. I also noticed most of the medical staff wearing something like a handkerchief or some type of cloth over their mouth and nose. I asked one of the nurses about it, and she said that it keeps out the smell and keeps blood from entering your mouth and nose during an amputation.

The more I thought about it and how it could possibly help in other areas, I decided to approach the head surgeon. I told him what I had found out and that it might be possible this could slow down the spread of diseases. I wasn't surprised when he didn't really believe me or pay any attention, so I sent a letter to Doctor Shaw and explained my findings.

We were already on our way to Camp Conway when I got his letter back. He said, "Dear Nurse Annie, once again your work in the field is most impressive, and here's what I've come up with. I agree that having a face covering would reduce the risk of catching diseases and greatly reduce the smell from gangrene and rotting flesh. Here's what I want you to do: when you get to your next camp, get the ones that are sick to wear a mask over their faces and keep a journal to see how much, if any, this helps the patients and fellow soldiers. Then you must let me know your findings. Once again, I am always proud of you."

Even growing up, Doctor Shaw was always like a father figure to me and really pushed me to do what I am doing. He didn't treat me like a young child, but as a student and protégé. I quickly came to appreciate and absorb his teachings. He is an older gentleman in his late 40s, single, with no children. He stood about six feet tall, with brown hair and green eyes. I must admit that I had a crush on him but never pursued it. When I asked him why a handsome man like him was not married, he told me that his wife died during childbirth and he never wanted to go through that again. I saw the pain in his eyes and felt truly guilty for asking him.

Finally Arrived

When we finally arrived at Camp Conway, I found out that your unit was there. I was excited but still too afraid to approach you. I saw that you were always busy teaching the new recruits how to fight and survive this war. When I looked at the new men, they looked like boys, and I wondered if we had lost so many men that we now had to resort to using children. I was absolutely angry at the thought that we were sending boys to do the fighting now. Even though I was angry, it wasn't my place to question it, but I knew that I would be seeing them in the next battle.

The camp here is quite comfortable. We have our own rooms, an outhouse for every two women. We had salted pork or salted beef to eat for dinner and supper, and for breakfast we have eggs and either donuts or flapjacks. The only interaction we have with the soldiers is when they come in complaining of being sick. I think some only come in to get out of performing their duties of the day. I usually report them to their commanders, but the ones that are truly sick—I took Shaw's advice and had them wear masks. I kept an eye on them and noticed how they seemed to recover a little bit quicker than the others.

Daily Routine

My daily routine wasn't much different from that of the other camps I have been at. Usually up by 5 a.m. and getting breakfast by 6.

Around 7 a.m., I report to the hospital to start my daily duties. Since I'm not on a battlefield, my days are usually boring. I clean and wash the sheets and put them on a clothesline so they will be dry by the next day. I do that until around noon. I stop to eat lunch and usually go back to my room and take a nap. I check back in with the doctors around 2 p.m., and if nothing is going on, then I am free for the rest of the day. But if we're busy dealing with a lot of sick patients, I am there until around 7 p.m. After supper, I go back to my room. When I have night watch, I stay in my room and sleep all day. Night watch isn't bad at all—everyone's asleep, sometimes me too—and I just have to try to keep the sicker ones comfortable.

Death of Mom

While there, I received a letter from my Aunt Debby. It read:

"I hope and pray that this letter finds you well. I have the responsibility to tell you that your mother has died. When she found out about your father's death, she stopped eating and would barely drink anything. Doctor Shaw did his very best to save her, but he said that she's dying from a broken heart and that the only one who can bring her back is herself. I have already made the proper arrangements to have her buried. Your uncle and I will remain here to watch over things until you can get home. I don't want you to worry about things—just your survival.

With much love,

Debby"

I sat in my room and cried, but I knew that this was coming. I walked up to Lizzy with tears in my eyes and told her that Mom had died. She gave me a big hug, and we both cried together. I was given the chance to leave here and go back home for good to take care of things, but I refused. Lizzy begged me to go, but I couldn't. There was nothing left for me there. Dad had all those properties, but I had already decided that I would sell them, move to Georgia, and become Mrs. Annie Calloway. The only problem is that you weren't aware of my existence—or my plan—yet.

My heart still reeling from loss, duty called us once again to the front lines.

Flintlock Valley

When we received word that we were getting ready to head toward a place called Flintlock Valley, there was something inside me that truly made me nauseous. I was still crying every day from the loss of my father and mother, and now we were about to go back into battle. For the first time, I was really scared. Maybe it was because this was the first time since their deaths, or the fact that I was getting really tired of all the death and carnage. I don't know, but I had a bad feeling about this one.

We left camp the next morning and were already aware of the fighting taking place. We got there that same day and jumped right into the fire. I quickly started helping to hold men down while limbs were being amputated and assisted in the stitching of wounds. I was still really scared for some reason but wasn't quite sure why. I had to put my fears aside for the moment to accomplish my mission, which was to save as many lives as possible.

It felt like an endless sea of bloody soldiers coming in. We were starting to get overrun by the number of wounded arriving at the field hospital. The screams were traumatizing, and a few of the nurses went into shock, so I had to slap them back into reality. It was nonstop all morning long. When I finally got a moment, I went out back to get the blood out of my hair. I broke down in tears and started to cry, thinking about what I was going to do. That's when I finally met you.

I was so embarrassed about how I looked, but you just smiled and lit up my world. I trembled with nerves when you spoke, and I knew then that my heart was gone forever. I prayed several times a day that you would be safe.

But just as fate brought us together, war tore me away once more.

Chapter 8: Capture

I stayed another day to scavenge around for any supplies that I could find. Now, understand that I had no intention of returning home. So, I started walking, hoping to find another unit to join. I know I promised her, but if I accidentally came across a unit on my way home, then oh well.

I have been walking for several days now, avoiding Confederate patrols and running desperately low on food. I came across this small town and wanted to go into town to get supplies and food. I was completely unaware that it was controlled by Confederate troops. I waited in the woods just outside of town until it was dark before trying to go into town and into the local saloon to find some food and water.

I was just about to make my move when I heard a pistol cock behind me. I instantly froze and started praying. I stood up and turned around to see a Confederate officer standing there. He asked what I was doing there, why I was there, and how many more were with me. I told him that I was alone and was looking for food and water, just trying to get back home to my family. I told him that I got shot at Flintlock Valley and couldn't use my left arm much, so I had to return home. He said, "That won't be possible because you are now my prisoner."

Interrogations and Beatings

I kept waiting for the right moment to take this man's life. That moment never came for me. Shortly after he captured me, I was standing in front of a Confederate intelligence officer. He asked me the usual questions, like who I was, what unit I was with, and how many more spies were out there. Now, the word "spy" scared me because the punishment for that is death. I would've been upset if I died by a firing squad over a misunderstanding. I quickly came to my defense on that one. I explained that I wasn't a Northern spy and that I got shot at Flintlock Valley and was trying to get home. I was only searching for some food and water. After several exhausting hours of interrogation, he said that he didn't think I was a spy and declared me a prisoner of war.

They put me in the town's jail and beat me for quite a long time. I was in shackles and chains, so I had no way to defend myself. Their jail cell was dark and musty; I could hear rats running across the floor and could feel the maggots on my legs. I was shackled to the door of the cell. Because they thought I would run away, they wouldn't take me to the outhouse, so I ended up using the bathroom on myself. Now, I am covered in blood and piss. It's almost daylight, and the mornings have gotten warm. They gave me a really thin blanket infested with lice, and the "food" was a type of soup filled with maggots. I was in terrible pain from the beating, but I wasn't going to show it. I stayed there for a few days before the wagon came to get me and take me to a prisoner of war camp.

They made sure that my time with them wasn't going to be an easy one. I was beaten twice a day to ensure that I wouldn't have the strength to fight back or try to escape. My shoes were taken from me when I got to the jail, and they put broken glass in front of the cell and outside in front of the window to keep me from trying to escape that way. After that first night, they stopped bringing me any type of food. I'm not complaining, actually; it's hard watching your food try to run away while trying to eat it.

The guards weren't happy about being there either. That was actually not a good thing because they took their anger and frustrations out on me. So, I made sure to be quiet and behave as much as I could, hoping that they would leave me alone, but that never worked. The beating the second night was the worst one. They came and got me and tied me to a tree. They proceeded to hit me with a leather horse strap about 15 times. Then, when they untied me, they started kicking and punching me. When they took me back to my cell, they dragged me across the broken glass, trying to cut me up even more.

The next morning, I woke up to a punch in the face. The guard grabbed me and took me outside for what I thought was another beating. Instead, there was a prisoner transport wagon there. They threw me in and shackled me down. I didn't know where I was going, but I knew that it had to be better than this place.

Chapter 9: Camp Brit Nessa

I am not quite sure how long we had been in those wagons, but it felt like forever. When we finally got to where we were going, it was the strangest-looking place I had ever seen. It looked like two giant brick buildings connected by a long tunnel. Each building appeared to be two stories tall, with very few windows and about 100 feet long. The whole camp itself was about a couple of acres total. There were guard posts about every 20 feet or so, each manned by two men, both carrying several flares. The fact that they had flares seemed strange, but they had a practical use. The guards would shoot them off at random intervals to keep a check on the yard.

The Gates

Well, because of that, it would make escape, for most people not a possibility. They also had several guard dogs as well. The dogs were a mix of German Shepherd and hound. When we got to the gate, they brought each dog over to smell each one of us so that, if we tried to escape, the dogs could pick up our scent. We were lined up single file and had to pass through a second gate manned by soldiers with loaded weapons and their fingers on the trigger. Once we passed through this second gate, numbers were placed on our arms. That told us what line we had to get into; my number was 4. The main reason for the numbers was to make it easier to keep track of the prisoners. The camp was broken down into four specific areas.

Numbering Systems

For instance, Area 1 represented the prisoners who attended to the needs of the guards or comandante. This area housed the personal servant prisoners of the staff. They took care of the cooking and cleaning for the guard staff. They were responsible for washing uniforms and keeping the barracks clean. That also included maintaining the horses and wagons. If they failed in any way or tried to eat any of the food, they were immediately taken to the courtyard and shot.

Section 2 housed the ones who were wounded but still able to perform daily chores. These men were responsible for keeping the camp and courtyard clean. They also tended to the grass in and outside the camp. This was a position many of the men wanted because it was a relatively easy job. The days were simple, and if it was raining, they stayed in the barracks all day. There were times I wished my wounds were bad enough.

Section 3 was for the prisoners who got in trouble for various reasons. For example, one prisoner was there because he dropped a rock while cleaning up the yard. Another was there because he didn't "properly" clean the outhouse. The amount of time you spent there was determined by the offense. It was a small, dark building with no windows and a small hole for air. It could hold up to 10 people at a time. So, if something happened and you were the unlucky number 11, you got locked up along the gate wall. There you would stay until your punishment was finished.

Section 4 housed the specialty workers. These were the ones responsible for the maintenance of the camp. This included maintaining the fences and the guard towers. These jobs were given to the ones who could be trusted the most. Even though we could be trusted, it was still a dangerous role.

We were told that there was only one rule—do as you're told and you will be alright. We stayed there for several days going through different types of testing for all sorts of diseases, as well as psychological and physical ability tests. It was horrible. People were sent into the common area of the complex in mass quantities. When it was full, the doors were shut. Then the people were shot and killed. When it was over, a person came out and spoke with a deep, growling voice. He said, "My name is Gen. Peterson; I am the commander of this fine facility here at Camp Brit Nessa, Alabama. You just witnessed what happens to those who do not do or understand what they are told. We do not tolerate rioting or protesting in any form or fashion here. THERE IS ONLY ONE RULE AND ONE RULE ONLY!" Everything was quiet after the incident, but people were still very jumpy around the guards.

Just when I thought the worst was over, we were relocated.

Camp Raleigh

We stayed here for about another week or so before we were moved to a second camp, Camp Raleigh. This is where I found out that one of my dear friends had been killed in the riot at the previous camp. This camp was a lot like the other one, except that instead of being separated, we were all placed into one general area. This one was a lot smaller than the first place we were at.

By this time, a lot of people were starting to get rebellious and aggressive. We were again separated into different areas. At this point, a few of the guys and I started to think of some way to get out of there. Before we could really establish a plan, some of the men were taken out to a field behind one of the wooden shacks and were executed for what the General considered to be treason. At that point, the rest of us decided to lay low for a while. The nice thing about this second location was that there were not nearly as many people here. Still, the one question on everyone's mind was why we were here and what happened to the rest of the people at the first camp. For several days, I would ask the guards what had become of the people at the first location, but as expected, nobody could—or would—answer my questions.

I came to realize pretty quickly that I was getting in well with the guards. All of us had our daily list of chores, and mine were usually pretty simple. For example, all I had to do was make sure that all the bunks in our building were made up correctly and that the floor was clean. You have to understand that we only had about ten people in our building. So, to have this job was everyone's wish. The rest of the time, I would be put in charge of the other details.

All I had to do was make sure the others had water, and when a bathroom break was needed, I would ensure that no one tried to escape. Every time someone went to take a leak or something, I so badly wanted to tell them to run, but I knew that if that happened, it would lead to my death as well. That was a chance I was not willing to take—at least not at this point. It was still too early in this thing to take that kind of risk. It became quite clear that the other prisoners looked up to me for strength and guidance, so I couldn't let them down. I don't know why they thought I could get them out of here, but they did. I didn't ask for what was about to happen—but it did.

Why Didn't They Listen

Against my gut feeling and logic, some of the prisoners decided that they had a better chance at survival by overpowering some of the guards and getting their hands on weapons. I told them repeatedly that it would not work because the guards were too powerful, but they didn't listen. One of the prisoners said they needed me to come with them; I told them I wouldn't because it would fail and they would surely die. To my disbelief and horror, about twenty of them went ahead and tried to get away. For a brief moment, I really thought they had a chance. It was pretty easy for some of them to take over the first couple of guards, because they were caught by complete surprise.

Now the one thing that the guards feared the most was happening—prisoners with weapons in their hands. The whole thing hinged on making sure that none of the guards could sound the alarm. Well, one of them did. Everyone who was not involved quickly ran for cover. The rest were slaughtered within a matter of minutes. It was horror of the highest magnitude. The guards showed no mercy and didn't let them die quickly. The screams of agony and despair were beyond any words that could describe it. Some were shot in the legs or arms, others were gutted by bayonets until their insides looked like noodles. Then the remaining survivors were dragged into the main yard for all to see.

The screaming went on until morning—about five to six hours—and each person died in a different way. The remaining ones who were still alive were taken to the main courtyard. There, they were tied to a log and placed over an open fire. The fire was not hot enough to kill, but hot enough to burn them without any kind of mercy. When the guards had their fill of that, they placed them on top of fire ant beds. Just outside the main gate were three giant fire ant beds, at least two feet tall and about four feet around. That is where they were finally allowed to die.

All this incident did was create more hatred toward the people who held us captive and deepen the feeling of desperation. On the other hand, what it didn't create was the level of fear the guards were after. The one thing we had on our side was that we knew how to make the lives of the guards miserable. Believe it or not, I was actually a very quiet person, so when I did do something, it was quite a spectacle.

There was no doubt that everyone, including myself, was too scared or nervous to think about trying anything for a while—but it didn't take long to get over that.

Still, I found solace in memories—of home, family, and Annie.

Chapter 10: Just Yesterday

It now seems so long ago when my brothers and I were running around on our homestead, where we would—and could—spend countless hours swimming and, of course, fighting all day. In the summertime, all of us could be found down at the pond, either swimming or fishing the days away. I am the next-to-youngest child, and I always caught all kinds of grief because of that. I guess the main reason was that I was almost killed as a child by a runaway horse. After that, my mother in particular always babied me, and my siblings did not like that.

I had walked into town that morning, as usual, to see a friend of mine when, out of nowhere, a horse came flying around the corner and hit me head-on. It happened so fast that I did not have time to react. The doctor told my parents that I was lucky to be alive. I had broken my left arm and leg, cracked three of my ribs, and suffered a pretty bad head injury. Not bad for a day's activities.

As I sit here in this prisoner of war camp in hot and humid Mobile, Alabama, all of that seems so far away. Thinking about my childhood and my precious Annie makes me feel better and sad at the same time because all there is around here is a bunch of doom and gloom. The smell of death is at every corner, and the stench of vile hatred is consuming the mind. I do not know exactly where we are; I just know that it is extremely hot in the summer. I have been here for a couple of months now, and I am still mourning the loss of my brothers-in-arms. I have not heard anything about my beloved Annie, but I fear the worst for her as well. To be honest with you, I do not know why I am still alive. Most of the people captured—when, or if, they try to escape—are killed on the spot. At this point, I wish that had happened to me.

Yesterday, I was put on burial detail. The more people I buried, the angrier I got. The conditions around here are disgraceful. If we're lucky, we get one slice of half-rotted meat and one mold-infested roll every day. After a couple of days of not eating and being worked to the point of collapse, you forget how nasty the food is, and you just eat it anyway. There is not a doctor on site (at least not for us), so most of the ones who have died have died from very treatable problems. One guy (whom I won't name out of respect) died from a stomach disease that could have easily been treated. Another died from a simple bee sting. I could go on for days about the death rate around here. Malaria and dysentery are very common because there are no sanitary places here. To me, the lack of food is the worst part of it all.

After getting caught trying to escape the first time, I have been watched and beaten every day. I guess that is the only reason I was kept alive: to be used as an example to everybody else. I am guarded every minute of the day, and at night, I am chained to my bed at the hands and feet. They also put a wooden beam across my chest so I cannot get a comfortable sleep. One thing I have learned about these guards: they are not much brighter than the others. What they have failed to realize is that the beam on me has actually made my heart and lungs stronger. I will need that extra strength on my next escape attempt. Come on now—did you really think this was going to stop me from trying again? You underestimate me. On days that we are not working, I am kept in my shackles the entire day. The problem I am going to have on this next attempt will be getting help from the other POWs.

The guards may not be bright, but they are meaner. The reason this attempt will be more difficult is that the other prisoners are afraid of them. They are more brutal and creative with their discipline techniques. One guy backtalked one of the guards and had his tongue cut off. That was so he would think twice about backtalking a guard.

That is just one of the things they do to the prisoners to keep them in line and under control. The only thing the guards have going for them is their level of intimidation. The average height is about 6 to 6 ½ feet tall, and they weigh about 230–250 lbs. on average. What the guards lack in brains, they make up for in size. That will be my biggest obstacle in the next attempt, and I assure you, there will be another attempt. All that will do is make me more creative with my plans, and I will also have to be very selective in whom I choose for this. But after what happened with Michelle, it might be safer for me to do this alone. I have made sure to keep a very low profile lately. I don't need to be raising any type of suspicion for myself, because any sign of an attempt will be met, I am sure this time, with death.

Kitchen Duty and The Laxative

The other day, I was put on kitchen detail. That got me in serious trouble for two reasons. The first was that I got caught giving real food to some of the weaker prisoners. I had lost so much weight that I was easily able to fit extra food into my pants and shirt and get it out that way. It wasn't like any of the guards weren't getting fed; as a matter of fact, there was a whole lot of food being thrown away every night. So, I politely helped myself a little bit. I paid for that one with "sun detail." What that is: I had to stand in the middle of the compound where there are no trees or any type of shade and "guard" the sun. Now, that may not seem like a hard thing to do, but when you are standing in the same spot from dawn to dusk with no water, it can be a "fun" experience. Did I forget to mention that the temperature easily hits over 100 degrees every day? The whole point of that little excursion was to prevent me from trying anything like that again—but it didn't work.

The second thing that got me in serious trouble was the invention of the bottled liquid poop. I found a way to make a homemade laxative that would have a person on the toilet for several days. It was a mixture of several different herbs and spices that created one heck of an internal explosion. It was quite comical to watch the reactions of the guards running to the outhouses and crapping all over themselves in the process. Sometimes the trouble you can get into is really quite worth the effort. I had only one goal, and that was to cause as much havoc as I possibly could without getting myself seriously hurt or killed. It didn't take the guards long to figure out that I was the one causing all of the trouble. It wasn't every day that I would do something like that to them because that would make it way too obvious. One thing I was good at was being able to create chaos and mayhem. You learn that stuff growing up with siblings as mean as mine were to me.

When I finally got caught, not only did I have to drink the stuff myself, I was given the job of cleaning out the outhouses—by hand. I grew up cleaning outhouses at home as a child. In the winter or the cooler months, it wasn't that bad, but in the summer, they were covered in flies and maggots, and I would throw up at least once. The only advantage of cleaning the outhouses—which, by the way, were just for the guards—was that when the laxative would hit, I was already there. Very convenient.

Chapter 11: The First Attempt at Escape

By this time, all of us had come to the conclusion that if we did not get free, we would all die out here. I met a girl by the name of Michelle, and we hit it off rather quickly. Like me, she had lost family and friends in the war. It wasn't long before we came up with an escape plan. After careful planning and plotting, we timed the rotation of the guards, the route of the dogs, and the sequence of the change in guards. We also knew that capture meant certain death.

After about a month of reconnaissance, we were ready to make our move. The plan was to escape through the number four entrance at the south end of the complex. We chose this one because it was the least guarded, and the supplies came through this entrance. Getting to and out the gate was the easy part. Making it past the first two hundred yards—now that was the "fun" part. The supplies always came in either at three in the morning every other Monday or nine at night every other Thursday. We decided to pick the three-in-the-morning route. We were now ready to escape. During the week prior, we made sure to hide rations at various points in our assigned areas of physical enhancement and development. This drew some attention from the guards, but our luck was that they were so confident nobody could escape, it didn't matter to them.

Now or Never

The day of the escape had come, and we had backup plans for our backup plans. The one thing we didn't count on was the tornado that came in the day before—and the extra guards because of it. The thought crossed our minds about waiting, but the longer we waited, the better the chances of getting caught or snitched on. We made sure that not a sound of this leaked out, but Michelle overheard some other people planning an escape themselves. The problem with that was, if they went first and got caught, the chances of us getting out would be slim to none. So regardless of the risk, we had to do it tonight.

The morning of the escape, we were both on edge. The day couldn't have been any prettier. The sky was a bright blue, there were no clouds, and the temperature was a perfect 77 degrees. As the day wore on, Michelle "grew" sick and was taken to the nurse and then to her room. Once she got back, she made sure all of the survival equipment was in order and ready to go. I made sure none of the guards suspected us by spreading a rumor that an attack on the commander was to happen at supper by way of poisoning. Of course, that wasn't going to happen, but the plan worked. With the guards on high alert, you'd think a person wouldn't even dream of escaping. Remember, I told you the guards were arrogant—they weren't paying any attention to the things we were doing. All of the guards' attention was at the mess hall and not on the gates, as it usually was. The time had come, and the move was now.

But before we could take that first real step toward freedom, there were two key obstacles we had to consider.

The Bridge

Before I can really get into the escape, there are a few things you must understand. The first is about the bridge, and the second is about the gate.

Let's start with the bridge. The bridge was a single-lane structure barely wide enough to get supply wagons across. It was laced with enough explosives to send a person to the moon, just in case anything got past the gate itself. It was also lined with two guards on each end and guards in the towers at the entrance to the gate. Swimming the moat was out of the question. Even if you made it past the barrage of gunfire from the guards, there were the alligators—and the snakes, which really turned me off to the whole idea of swimming. It was about 75 to 100 feet in length, and everything around it was kept from growing so that the area remained easily visible.

The Gate

The main obstacle in our plan was getting past the gate itself. The gate would be an impossible feat unless you could "catch a ride" underneath a wagon. The gate stood about ten feet tall and three feet thick (so explosives could not penetrate it), and fifteen feet across. It was primarily made of wood with metal crossbeams throughout its interior. It was designed to withstand any military bombardment.

Once you got through the gate, it was wide open from there. But don't be fooled—just because it was open didn't mean it was going to be easy. There was no way of knowing where the next town was or where the next source of food or water would come from. Without any contact with the outside world, there was no way to get this information—or if we could, we didn't know if it could be trusted.

We Are Out

As usual, the supply wagons showed up at their appointed time. Michelle and I met up at the south gate, about twenty feet from the entrance. We waited with nervous anticipation while the wagon was unloaded and turned around. Finally, it started to move, so we made our move. After a lot of careful planning, the time was now, and we had crossed the point of no return. Somehow, we managed to elude the guards as we ran and climbed onto the back of the wagon. Once we cleared the gate, we would have to jump off and make our way to the rendezvous point—quickly. We knew it wouldn't take long for the guards to figure out we were missing, and they would surely come looking for us.

We made it past the guards at the gate much more easily than we had expected. It was probably because they never expected anyone to try to escape. The arrogance of the guards was truly their Achilles' heel. Michelle and I finally reunited at the rendezvous point and took off from there. We ran about one or two miles before deciding to stop for a minute. Just because we escaped the compound didn't mean we were safe. We stayed hidden in a cornfield for about an hour, resting and listening for any signs of someone following us. Once we were convinced that nobody was around, we decided it was time to get out of there.

We knew our escape was only the beginning—survival came next.

The thing that both of us were most concerned about was accidentally getting turned around and heading back toward the compound. That wouldn't be hard to do, considering it was still dark and we really didn't know where we were going.

The Farmhouse

Another problem we knew we'd have was finding regular clothes and shedding these gaudy uniforms. And when I say gaudy, I mean it. The pants were dark blue, and the shirt was white and orange—at least two sizes too large. Of course, that was probably to keep people from escaping. They were made out of some type of cotton material that, when you sweat, clings to your body, making movement an effort in futility. We knew that no matter how far we got, we'd never truly get away unless we got out of these uniforms.

We had been walking for the rest of the night when we finally found a farmhouse off by itself. We approached with much fear and caution because we didn't know who or what might be there. We grew nervous at the lack of noise. There were no barking dogs—no sounds at all, for that matter. We walked up to the front door and listened for any sounds coming from inside—there were none. I finally got the nerve to break down the front door. To our surprise, the door was unlocked, as if someone were expecting company or something.

We looked around the house for anybody, but no one was to be found. Then we went outside to the barn—and that's where we found the husband and his wife. Dead. They had both been shot once in the back of the head. What scared us the most was that, if we were caught and traced back here, we would be killed for the murder of these two.

We quickly found some clothes that fit us a lot better than the prison uniforms. We sat there for about two or three more hours, grabbed all the food we could carry, and hit the road. Much to our surprise, we had not heard any sounds of dogs barking or the screaming of guards. Were they just playing a game of cat and mouse, or were they even searching for us at all? The eerie silence was the worst part of it all. Here we were, out in the middle of nowhere, with no clue where we were or where we were going, and no signs of life anywhere. It was almost like we were in some kind of ghost town. By the time nightfall came, we were both exhausted from the day. We found a small (and yet again abandoned) house where we hunkered down for the night. I didn't get much sleep that night. Every waking moment, I was expecting to get caught or hear the guards coming for us—they never did. To me, that was the worst part of it all: not knowing what to expect around the next corner.

It has now been about a week, and we are still on the run. There have been no signs of an attempt to recapture us, and nobody seems to notice that we are gone. I don't know if that is a good thing or not. I can't help but wonder: have we actually managed to get away and are now free from these people? That feeling of freedom was to be short-lived.

Michelle and I were sitting by a tree one afternoon when four guys came out of nowhere. As soon as I saw them, I pushed Michelle off to the side and tried to wrestle the men off me. That was definitely an effort in futility. They injected a needle in my arm that immediately rendered me totally incapable of any resistance. The last thing I remember is seeing Michelle running off into the woods.

What Did You See

I woke up in a room that was quite busy with soldiers and other personnel. They had me tied to a chair in front of a desk, and I had no clue how long it had been. It wasn't too long after I woke up that a soldier came over and sat down at the desk. I will never forget what he said. He said, "My name is General Peterson, commander of this facility. You have been brought to me because you and a female friend have escaped from us." All I could think about was killing him. I knew I couldn't—not in my condition, not with all the soldiers around. Still recovering from whatever they'd injected me with, I made a vow: before I die, I'll kill him. That promise kept me alive through things that should've ended me.

My next obvious question was what happened to Michelle. All he would say was that she was "taken care of," and she wouldn't be trying that again. One thing I had already learned is that you can't take these people at face value. What they say and what they mean are usually two totally different things.

The question is: did they kill her, or did they send her away to another camp far from here? I don't know, but I will find out what happened to her. He seemed to be more interested in what we had seen outside the gates than the actual escape itself. He kept asking me where we stayed and how we managed to keep from getting caught. I know I really pissed him off when I told him that the escape was easy because his guards were idiots. They noticed us planting supplies and other essentials several times and didn't even ask any questions.

The only time I began to get nervous was when he started asking about the two dead people we found. I was certain we were going to get blamed for their deaths. It was almost like he had never seen the outside world, based on the way he was acting. His questions were oddly specific, considering he was asking about the death of two civilians outside his military jurisdiction. He kept asking how they were killed and how long I thought they had been dead. Out of all the questions he asked, there were two that really struck me as strange. The first was: what position were they in? And the second was: were they naked?

At this point, I began to think that either he had something to do with the murders, or he already knew about them and wanted to know what I knew. If he did know about them, I was convinced he would try to tag the blame on me. Even through all the questioning, I still couldn't get it out of my mind—what happened to Michelle? That was more gut-wrenching than anything else. I couldn't stop wondering if she was alive or dead.

You Betrayed Me!!

After a few days in the prison at the compound, I found out that Michelle was still alive. I was really relieved to hear that news! I was even more excited when I finally saw her, but the excitement was short-lived. I found out that the guards had been following us the entire time because Michelle befriended me to earn her freedom!! Everything she told me was a lie to earn my trust. Her family was never killed, and she never went through any of the stuff she claimed. I also found out that she was sent to the camp to keep an eye on me because my reputation as a troublemaker had preceded me.

I can't believe I trusted her, and I can't believe I actually let my guard down and believed her. It was like a knife had been stabbed into my soul. Now, understand that I only became friends with her to get out and get back to my Annie. She proved that I couldn't trust or believe anyone here, so I must work on getting out of here alone. I worked on my plan for several weeks, but something happened that made my plan no longer a possibility: April 9, 1865.

And just like that, the war that had shattered millions of lives—including mine—finally ended.

Chapter 12: The Journey Home

It's Over!

April 9, 1865, Robert E. Lee surrenders to Ulysses S. Grant at Appomattox Courthouse in Appomattox, Virginia, officially ending the bloodiest conflict this country has ever seen.

I'm sitting here in this prisoner-of-war camp just outside of Mobile, Alabama. I've only been here a relatively short time now, and I must admit, I have it pretty easy here. When I arrived, I was put in charge of making sure that the other prisoners were doing what they were supposed to be doing. Really simple job, because most of the men, including myself, are too weak to cause any problems. This is a very small camp—only a couple hundred prisoners here—and the warden of the camp and the guards are quite pleasant to be around. We have three meals a day and on-site doctors that can handle anything.

We Are Free

One day we were called into formation and told that the war was over and that we were free to go home. All of the prisoners started to celebrate. I looked around, and there were no guards to be found. My very first thought was that I actually survived this war. Even though the war was over, the threat of death still remains around every corner.

Most of the prisoners started sprinting towards their homes without any thought of survival or food. I expect most of them to be dead within a week or two. I gathered up any food and supplies that I could find and carry. I grabbed an extra pair of shoes and some socks for the long journey home, so I began walking. My guess is that it's going to take at least six weeks to get home, and possibly longer. I'm hoping to get there before the weather gets too hot. I'm extremely weak, so I'm sure I will be walking slow. My main fear is that some of the Confederates may not be aware that the war is over, and I could once again find myself in the same situation—except this time, I have no way to defend myself.

I've been walking for about a week now, and so far haven't run into any Confederate soldiers. I've limited myself to just a few bites a day from the salted pork I took from the camp. Water hasn't become a problem yet because I try to stay near any creeks that I might come across. My thoughts are constantly on my beloved Annie. I can still taste her kisses and feel her soft touch. Every night she's my last thought, and every morning my first. Her eyes are like a beacon guiding me back to her side. Only God knows what tomorrow will hold.

Three Confederates

My thoughts of Annie were interrupted when I came across three Confederate soldiers. My heart stopped beating. I quickly ran and hid in the bushes, hoping that I wasn't seen. At this point, I didn't know if they were aware that the war was over, and if they were, how they would react to my presence. Would they just pass me by? Would they take out their frustrations and hatred on me? With no way to defend myself, I was truly afraid.

They quickly spotted me and ordered me out of the bushes. Having no idea what I was walking into, I offered no resistance to their orders. I don't know who was more scared at that moment—me or them. I was thankful when I found out that they knew the war was over and, like myself, just wanted to get home. I could see in their eyes that they were crushed, their souls shattered by the loss of the war.

Even though I didn't have it to spare, I offered the three of them some of my salted pork. It was now getting close to sundown by this point, so we decided to set up camp in an open field for the night. Being in an open field on a night with a full moon was a great idea. We could see anything or anyone that was trying to approach us. We just sat there and talked for several hours about our homes and our families. We talked about some of the battles we were involved in, and I was surprised when I found out that they were also at Sultan's Crossing and Flintlock Valley. There was no animosity toward each other, and we shared a few laughs.

Since I became a prisoner of war, I haven't heard anything about the whereabouts of Annie or even if she's still alive. I can't handle the thought of her being dead—I had to very quickly put that thought out of my head. She's the driving force behind my survival.

Clark

Of the three men—Clark, Morris, and Holstead—Clark was the one that made me nervous and a little bit scared. Every time he looked at me, he had that "I'm going to kill you in your sleep" glare in his eyes, and in my weakened state, he could easily overpower me. If he tried, what would the other two Confederates do about it?

There's something off about Clark. That's what worries me. He seems to be the bully of the bunch and the troublemaker. He's over six feet tall with brown hair and hazel eyes. He grew up on the streets of Baton Rouge and learned how to fight at a very young age. When he was four years old, his parents up and abandoned him. The orphanage took him in, but he was always a violent person. When the war broke out, he finally felt like he belonged somewhere.

I noticed his uniform has what seems to be fresh blood on it, along with cuts on his face, but I was too afraid to ask about it. I just assumed that he got cut up walking through some briars or something.

Morris

Morris was the smallest of the three. He was maybe five feet tall, lanky, with short red hair and a mustache. He went by Stubby instead of his real name and seemed to have the temper to go with it. He had this deep Southern accent that made me laugh. I was told that on the battlefield he was the most violent of them all. I honestly found that hard to believe, seeing the size of Clark.

He lived between New Orleans and the Gulf of Mexico. He talked often about spending his days on the beach and his love for the water, and I told him I was the same way. He got married just before leaving for the war and has a three-year-old son he hasn't even seen yet. His wife's name is Rebecca and she is the love of his life—and just like Annie's parents, they grew up together in New Orleans.

Holstead

Holstead was the most relaxed of the group. He's about my size—about 5'7", slender build, bald as a baby's bottom—and it struck me as odd how chilled he is. He said he has nobody waiting for him at home and plans on getting into the gambling business to make some serious money.

He told me that people can make easy money there by working in one of the many hotels or on a riverboat. A close friend of his owns a faro table and would let him work with him, maybe even get another one. He explained that's where the real money is.

They were hoping, as was I, to hopefully find a way to shorten the trip—either by train or carriage. We camped there for a couple of days just to get some much-needed rest. I knew that the longer I stayed, the longer it would take me to get home—and the longer I would be around Mr. Clark. The thought of them robbing me for my food and supplies was a constant worry in my mind. I wasn't sure if it was, as a few weeks ago, the fact that they were former enemy soldiers, or simply that there were three of them and only one of me.

Now Holstead and Morris were focused on getting home and were sick of the bloodshed and violence of war. I really think that, for Clark, the war will never be over. I feel that Holstead and I could be friends—he just wants to get home and start his life over again.

He told me about his depression because he couldn't understand how Lee could surrender. With tears in his eyes, he said, "Thank God that the bloodshed is over. Do you think that God will forgive me for what I've done?"

"Tony (Holstead), I feel the same way."

The Evil Within

With Holstead and Morris, I didn't worry about being asleep and suddenly waking up with a knife in my back—but Clark was a different story. There was always this feeling of absolute evil about him. He made two comments that really scared me to my core:

"You know that I could slit your throat and nobody would know," and

"I wonder how Yankee meat would taste cooked on an open fire?"

He truly scared me, and I always kept one eye on him at all times. I've never met anyone as purely evil as this man.

For obvious reasons, I didn't sleep much that night. I would wake at the slightest sound. I'm not entirely sure if it's because I'm still jumpy from all the combat, or because I didn't want my throat slit—or both. I woke up right at daybreak and began my journey home again.

My thoughts are always on my Annie, and not knowing what's happened to her is driving me absolutely crazy. My mind keeps running wild, and keeping it under control is getting more and more difficult with each passing day. So as soon as daybreak hit, I was gone.

And then came a distraction I didn't expect—an abandoned house with secrets of its own.

Abigail - The House

I'd been walking for about another day or so when I came across this really small farm. It looked completely abandoned. The windows were broken, and the grass was really high. It looked like an old, rundown shack that had been neglected for quite some time. There was a small barn just to the right of the house, and it was missing part of the roof. I could see some hay up in the loft, and on the bottom floor, I could see a horse trough that looked empty. There were pieces of wood that looked like they had rotted and fallen. The ladder up to the loft was broken in a couple of places. The floor of the loft looked like nearly every slat had holes in it. The horse stall looked like it was about the only thing in decent shape.

By this point, my curiosity had gotten the better of me. I couldn't help but wonder how and why this place had fallen into such disarray. I had to know what happened here. I moved to where I could get a better view of the inside of the house.

The house was nothing more than a three-room shack with a porch holding it up. The sitting area only had two chairs and a very small table in between. The floor was covered by nothing more than some wooden planks. The chairs looked very old, with the seat torn out of one. In front of them was a very small fireplace with a very small mantle on top. The walls were nothing more than wooden planks held together by dry clay. The kitchen was barely big enough to hold a small stove and table with two chairs. There were just a couple of pots and pans in the kitchen. The bedroom itself was only big enough for a small bed and a very small table. The only window had been busted out.

It Was a Trap

By now, I was almost completely out of food and water, and without any type of weapon, hunting or even catching fish was pretty much impossible. I walked up slowly toward the house and sat behind a tree for about 30 minutes or so, watching for any movement or sound. I was extremely cautious because I didn't know exactly what I was walking into. After sitting for about an hour total, I felt safe enough to approach it. I knocked a few times, and with no answer, I slowly opened the door, keeping my body shielded by the outside wall just in case. There was nobody inside. I walked around, and when I put my hand on the stove, I realized it was warm to the touch. My first and immediate thought was that I'd walked into a trap.

I instinctively went into combat mode. I was completely panicked. I grabbed a blanket and some bread that was on the table and started to leave.

I ran out the door, and when I got near the barn, I heard that all-too-familiar sound of the hammer on a rifle cocking. I just knew I was dead. I was madder at myself for falling for this than I was at whoever was on the other end of that rifle. They were defending their property—I was the intruder. I put my hands up in the air and looked around but didn't see anyone.

I said, "My name is James Calloway, and I mean you no harm. I have no weapons, and I'm really hungry and tired. I'm just trying to get home, so please don't pull that trigger."

After a few very intense moments, I heard the hammer of the rifle being put back into safe mode. I kept looking around for who and where this person was, but still no sound or sight. I kept looking, and this mystery person refused to show themselves.

Once again, I said, "My name is James Calloway. Please come out—I won't hurt you, I promise." My only guess was that it was a child or a single woman and they were too scared to come out.

She Finally Appears

Then, after a couple of minutes or so, I heard some movement coming from the barn loft. Out came this girl who looked to be only 18 or 19 years of age. Her blonde hair was all tangled, her dress was dirty and torn in several places, and she had several bruises on her face and arms. Her eyes were filled with fear. It was the same look I had seen thousands of times on the battlefield. Knowing that at any moment, she could pull that hammer back on that shotgun and actually pull the trigger this time, I stayed really still.

The very first thing I needed to do was get that shotgun not pointing in my direction. I knew I could easily overpower her, but there was no need for force or violence. Her hands were shaking, but with every move I made, her hands became steady and focused on me. She still hadn't said anything, so again I repeated my name and told her I wasn't going to hurt her. I asked her again what her name was, and finally, in a soft voice, she said her name was Abigail—but Abby for short.

I still didn't want to make any sudden moves because I still had a double-barreled shotgun pointed at my face. With a soft but firm voice, I said, "Abigail, I really need you to lower that weapon before either of us gets hurt. If you believe that I'm not going to hurt you, will you please lower that shotgun?"

Overwhelming Fear

She immediately started crying, so I stepped closer and took the shotgun away from her, then I put my arms around her. She melted in my arms, so I picked her up and took her inside, placing her on her bed. She immediately started screaming and trying to hit me. I took a few steps back, and she scurried over to the corner of the bed, cowering in fear.

"Abigail, I promise I'm not going to hurt you." I just turned around, left the room, and went outside to sit on the steps. After an hour, I went back inside, and she was still cowering in the corner of the bed, absolutely terrified.

I just stood there looking at her, and two thoughts came to mind. The first was that I could walk away, but my conscience wouldn't let me. I also had to show her she could trust me—just enough to let me help. I found some canned vegetables, and when the stove got hot enough, I made us supper.

I figured the only way she would begin to trust me was to prove that I wasn't a threat. When the food was ready, I took her a bowl of vegetables and some water from the well. She had a very small table next to her bed, and I placed the bowl and water there. I slowly backed away with my hands in the air. I didn't really understand why I had my hands up, but somehow, it felt necessary at that moment. I needed to find a way for her to trust me.

I grabbed my own bowl and inhaled it; I didn't realize how hungry I was. I saw her very slowly open the door, and I just sat there looking at her. It became clear that the girl I was looking at hadn't existed a few weeks ago. She'd gone through something very horrible. She opened the door a little bit more and looked at me, and behind those beautiful blue eyes was just a lifeless shell of a person.

I motioned for her to come sit down, but she slammed the door shut. I realized then that this would be a very slow process. A few minutes later, she opened the door again and said one sentence that shook me to my core:

"They also said that they wouldn't hurt me."

Then she shut the door again.

I wasn't quite sure how to respond at first. I told her through the door that I meant what I said and that I was going to sleep in the barn—and to come get me if she needed anything. I was so tired that I barely remember lying down.

She Finally Opens Up

When I woke the next morning, I found her asleep next to me in the barn. I feel like I'm beginning to gain her trust. I took my blanket, covered her up, and went to check things out. Abigail finally woke up and came out of the barn, but before I got a chance to even say anything, she went into the house without even looking in my direction. I wanted to follow her inside, but I thought that might not be the best idea right now. She came out to where I was working with a glass of water.

She asked me just two questions. The first was, "Why didn't you try to rape me like those other three men did?" and the second, "Why are you being so nice to me and helping me?" I simply told her, "I wasn't raised to mistreat a woman. I was raised to cherish them, and I could never physically hurt a woman. As for your second question, it's clear that you're very vulnerable here. Now I have a question for you— where are your parents?"

She said with tears in her eyes, "It happened about a week or so ago, when three Confederate soldiers came to our door. When my dad answered it, one of them punched him in the face. When he fell to the ground, one of them jumped on top of him and stabbed him in the heart, killing him. Two of them dragged my mother to the bedroom and violently raped her. I could hear the screams of pain and agony as they tortured her. When they finished with her, the third man, who was watching me to make sure I didn't try to escape, had his way with her. When they were all finished, they punched her several times and then snapped her neck.

They said that they weren't going to hurt me and that I could trust them. The next thing I know, I'm waking up in the barn, naked and covered with blood from where I was raped and sodomized. I laid there for about a day before I could even move. The pain was absolutely unbearable, and when I went to the bathroom, I would scream and cry at the top of my lungs. When I could finally move again, I put my dress back on and laid there and cried. After I got to where I could walk again, I dug a shallow grave to bury them in and cleaned up as much of the blood as I could."

They're Mine

My anger was so powerful, I grabbed the shotgun and her horse, and we went after them. We rode nonstop through the night until I found them a day later. I dropped her off close enough to hear, but far enough not to easily be seen. They were surprised to see me and asked how I got the horse. I wanted to make sure they were the ones who did this before I killed them for no reason. I told them that I got it at a really small farm about a few hours' ride north of here.

Holstead said that they stopped by there, but there was nobody around, so they left. Then I asked Clark how he got those scratches and cuts on his face. All he said was that it was none of my business. When he said that, Abigail came out from behind a nearby tree and said they were the men who did this. That was all I needed to hear. I shot both Clark and Holstead in the face, killing them instantly. I lost track of that weasel Morris until she yelled and pointed towards him, shouting, "He's getting away!" I quickly caught up to him and tackled him. I explained to him that the only reason he was still breathing was because of that baby boy, and that if I ever saw him again, I would kill him without hesitation and without remorse. I hit him in the face with the butt of the rifle. I grabbed a nearby rock that was heavy and slammed it on both his ankles, breaking them. I looked down at him and said, "Good luck getting home."

When all was finished, she came over and gave me a long kiss. I felt so guilty kissing her because I felt like I was cheating on Annie. We gathered up anything we could and headed back toward Abigail's farm. We rode all night, taking our time, and got back in the early morning hours of the next day. We slept outside underneath the stars. I woke up and saw that she wasn't there, so I walked around and saw her bathing in the creek. I quickly turned around and started walking back toward the barn to try to clean it up.

No, Absolutely Not

Now understand that I have no intention whatsoever of taking her with me. I spent the next several days there doing some cleaning and repairs. I wanted to make sure she had a safe place to live and a way to defend herself as well. I was able to repair the roof and seal off the windows that had been broken. I chopped up some wood and made other repairs. My biggest curiosity was: how did it get looking like this in just a matter of weeks? The grass I could understand, but not the barn or the house. I asked her about it. She said, "Dad got seriously injured from being thrown off a horse a year ago, and it broke his back. He never fully recovered, so Mom and I tried to take care of him and this place too, but it simply became too much to deal with."

The night before I was planning to leave, I explained to her that I needed to start heading back toward my home. She begged and pleaded with me not to leave her here alone again. I told her that it simply wasn't possible for her to come with me. She hugged me tight and only said three words: "Why, James, why?" The sadness and fear in her voice truly broke my heart. I was at a real crossroads. Taking her with me would put both of us at great risk, and I would now have to look after another person. Leaving her here welcomed certain death for her. After what I had done for her ran out, she'd have no way to defend herself. And what happens if more men show up after I leave?

Fine, You Can Go

We stayed up all night talking, and I fought all night, going back and forth inside my head and heart. Either way we go creates great risk for both of us. I've always been a practical person, and the thought of leaving her here alone was really bothering me. So, with great reluctance, I agreed to let her come with me. I'm not in the least bit happy about it, but it is the best option.

I explained to her that I wasn't fond of this idea, but I couldn't leave her alone either. The main condition for her coming with me was that, no matter what, she must do what I say, when I say it—without exception. There's a lot of danger out here and most of it can kill. Between the wild animals and chance encounters with returning Confederates who may not be so friendly, death lurks around every corner.

So, the next morning, she got the horse ready, and I went around gathering anything we could use to survive or use as a weapon. I secured and loaded the weapons; I had the shotgun and she had a pistol. We finished loading the saddlebags and started our journey. We got a few hundred yards down the road, and out of nowhere, she yelled, "James, stop! I need to do something before we get too far!"

"Abigail, you need to hurry. We really need to get going. What could be that important?"

When we got back to the house, she ran inside, and with the fire in the stove still burning, she lit a torch and set the house and the barn on fire. She talked me into standing there and watching them burn to the ground. She stood there with tears in her eyes and simply said, "Thank you. I needed to do that for me." After everything burned down, she gave me a big hug and said, "Now I'm ready to go. It's time to leave the horrors and pain of this place behind me. I buried my pain and sorrow inside that burning building. I'm ready for the next chapter."

I have to admit that I admire her strength and resolve. Even after witnessing the death of her parents and suffering the violent assault, she has held strong. Deep down, I think I needed her as much as she needed me at this moment in time. Don't get me wrong—my thoughts and heart are with my beloved Annie. My love for her is the only reason I was able to walk away from Abigail.

We've been on the road for a few days now. It's been a slow, aggravating few days. Due to her condition, we have to take several breaks, and she has to lie down a lot. There are times that I am beginning to regret this. We came across a small town called Salt. We stopped right outside of town, and I changed out of my uniform and put on a few of her dad's clothes. Not completely knowing what I was walking into, I thought it safer for me to go into town alone. She stayed hidden behind some bushes. I wasn't too worried at this point because she had a weapon and wasn't afraid to use it. I rode around for a little bit and went to pick her up.

She had some money that her dad had left her, so we had money for a hotel for a couple of nights. While she was waiting on me, she got friendly with a cat and wanted to keep it. I was kind of upset about it, but when I saw that smile on her face, I couldn't say no. It was a pretty cat—mainly white with a black "mask" across its face like a robber and a few other black spots. He had the prettiest green eyes I've ever seen on a cat.

"Doctor help!"

That first night, she woke up around 2 a.m. screaming in pain and agony. I went to get the doctor, and we took her to his office. While he was conducting his examination, I was trying to explain the situation to the local sheriff. He was going to put me in jail for the assault until Abigail told the sheriff that I was the one who rescued her. He asked what the men looked like, and I told him that he didn't need to worry about that because "I took care of the situation. They won't be bothering anyone anymore." He said that was good enough for him.

About 30 minutes later, the doctor came back in and said in a somber voice, "She won't survive the next 24 hours. The damage to her pelvic area is just too severe." He found several tears in the lining of her colon, and she was bleeding out internally. "There's no way for me to stop that much bleeding. I'm truly sorry, but there's no way to save her. The fact that she's lived this long is a testament to her courage and strength. She's resting right now; I gave her some morphine for the pain and to help her sleep."

"So, she only has a few hours left?"

"Maybe another 24 hours at the very most."

I told the doctor that I appreciated his efforts.

I can't help but feel guilty to some degree because if I had known the severity, we would've backtracked to Mobile, and maybe she would've survived. I took her back to the motel room and stayed up all night with her, holding her hand. The last time she opened her eyes, she looked at me and said, "Thank you for rescuing me, and even if you don't love me, I will always love you. You gave me a chance to survive, and for that I will always love you." I leaned down and gave her a kiss on the forehead and told her that I loved her too. Her eyes lit up, and with a smile on her face, she took her last breath—and then she died. I laid my head upon her stomach and cried.

I stayed around another couple of days so she could be buried. Even though this war is over, it's still taking lives. After the funeral, I went through her belongings and took out what was going to be of good use to me. The rest I took out behind the hotel and burned. All I kept was the remaining money and a locket that she was wearing when she died. Her death is affecting me more than I expected. I watched thousands and thousands die on the battlefield, and it never affected me like this. She will always have a special place in my heart.

I Need to Get Home

The next morning, I got on my horse, Abby (yes, I named the horse after her), and once again said goodbye to someone close to me. With Abby beneath me, I set my sights on home—obsessed with ending the pain and starting over. I'm not worried about food anymore; I have the means and the skill to hunt now—and especially the weapons to defend myself against animals and possibly people. I found out about the Lincoln assassination while in Salt. My heart was completely broken at the news, and I keep wondering: will this carnage ever completely end? Andrew Johnson was sworn in as the new president. I'm concerned about his plans to reunify the country.

As the road continued to stretch ahead, so did the dangers that came with it.

The Saloon Duel

Even though the days are longer and the weather is getting hotter, Abby and I are making good time. I'm hoping to be home in about a week or so. We made it to Columbus, Georgia without much incident. I made sure that anyone I came across, I either ignored or avoided any type of conversation. I stayed here for a couple of days so both of us could get some rest.

I was in a saloon the night I arrived, and while sitting there minding my own business, two men wanted to sit down. Now, I know from my own experiences that this isn't going to end well—for either them or me. I just politely said that I would rather be alone.

One of them sat down anyway and said, "I don't think that you heard us, stranger. We said that we want to sit down and chat with you." By now, I already had my pistol drawn and cocked, sitting in my lap. So I said, "No, you don't understand, you giant tub of lard. I said I want to be alone, and if you value your life, you would leave me alone now. I have a loaded pistol in my lap that's cocked and ready for action, and it's pointed at you right now. If your friend—who has decided to try to get me from behind—only knew that I also have a knife in my other hand that I'm going to kill him with as well, he would change his mind about his plan. So, what say you, my fat friend?"

They both smiled and said that they were only playing and meant no harm. But when I said that I wasn't playing and I would've killed them right here, they left the saloon.

My thoughts have been and always will be on my Annie until we can touch again. I'm not sure if she is dead or alive, or if she was involved in any more battles after we parted. I sent a telegram to my parents after my arrival here in Columbus. My parents were so excited, and my mom sent me money through a bank transfer so I could catch the train for the remainder of the trip. My mom sent me a simple text that read, "Welcome home, my precious child. I love you and will see you soon."

I admit that I really enjoyed the train ride for the rest of the trip home. The stable car was set up quite nicely as well. She had plenty of hay and was even fed apples as a treat. My food wasn't too bad—we had bread with fresh homemade strawberry jam and coffee. They had peanuts by the sackful, and that made me really happy. I filled my pockets full and sat back down for the remainder of the trip.

Seeing the devastation was the worst part of the ride home. Atlanta is literally a city of ashes, with very few buildings left in workable condition. The railroads are mostly destroyed, with just a few lines repaired enough to travel through. Almost all the citizens are homeless and try to find shelter anywhere they can, laying their heads wherever they can find a spot. There was only one building left that Sherman didn't destroy when he came through Atlanta, and that was a church. It has now been turned into a soup kitchen. Even outside of the city, the destruction is just as bad. The scorched-earth policy has left everything in complete ruins. I'm afraid of how my town will look when I get there.

Finally, Home

After three years of war, the loss of my very close friends, the physical and mental wounds, and the constant nightmares, I finally arrived home on June 28, 1865. I'm free now from the boredom and harsh demands of field life and now just want to get my life back.

When I arrived at the train station, all the family—except Patrick—was there to greet me. When I stepped off the train, my mother ran up and hugged me so tight that I thought I was going to pass out. All she could say was, "All my boys are home. Thank you, my Heavenly Father, thank you."

Everyone was as happy to see me as I was to see them. I asked about Patrick and where he was, and in a disgusted-sounding voice,

Mom said, "He's been banished from the family because his loyalties lay with the Confederacy and not the family. He did tell me what you did to him at Flintlock Valley. I didn't know who I was madder at—you or him."

"Do you not understand that what I did actually saved his life? Or do you even care? Listen, I've been gone for three years, lived through horrors that you can't even begin to imagine. Now you're going to tell me that you're mad at me for saving my brother's—your son's—life!? Let's just head back home."

I didn't really talk much on the way home. I tied Abby to the back of the wagon so she could enjoy the trip too without carrying much weight.

When we pulled into the property, I got out of the wagon and kissed the ground I was standing on. It felt like I had just walked into a different world. I went from sleeping in trenches to sleeping in a real bed. I truly couldn't believe after all this time—that I was actually finally home for good. As I lay in my bed, unable to sleep as usual, for the first time in three years it felt strangely comfortable. My thoughts now dwell on Annie and finding my brother Patrick.

Now to Find Patrick

I completely understand their embarrassment over what he did, but he's still family. After coming from a war that completely decimated so many families, what I don't understand is how they can hold on to this. It's going to be an uphill fight for me to heal until I can find my brother and get the family to forgive and forget.

My family is well known here in town, so I'm hoping that will make finding him just a little bit easier for me. The next morning, I left the house really early to begin my search for my brother. I thought the most logical place would be to go talk to the pastor first. Since everything revolved around the church, that would be a good place to start my search.

When I got to the pastor's house, he was chopping wood, getting ready for winter when it comes. He threw his axe down and ran over and gave me a big hug.

"You know that I spent a lot of time praying for my boys, and I'm so glad to see you are home now, safe and sound."

"Thank you, but I'm not here for pleasantries. I need to know if you've seen my brother Patrick."

"I saw him last week at the Colston farm."

"Wait a second, the Colstons? They are the ones who investigated and harassed our family prior to and during the war! And now you're saying that he's staying with them over there?"

I was in complete shock. It seems like he really has left the family behind. I'm not giving up on him because the trauma—and the fact that the family has betrayed him—is driving his decisions. He's having to accept that all the people he saw die have now died for no reason, and the punishment that the South will have to face will be a hard pill to swallow for him and all the Confederates as well.

The Colston family were the main ones turning in the families that were helping slaves escape and are responsible for many people losing their lives. As much as I don't want to, I guess that's where I'm heading next.

Fortunately for me, their farm is only a few miles from the pastor's. When I arrived there, I felt a lot of anger and hatred. I was very aware of my surroundings, and it seemed like everyone stopped what they were doing and was watching me as I went by. Several men armed with rifles made their way to the front steps of the house. Everyone was aware of the situation between my family and theirs, so nobody knew what my intentions were going to be.

Before I could even get to the door and dismount my horse, Mr. Colston came out.

I told him, "I'm not here to cause any trouble, sir. I just really need to know if you have seen my brother Patrick. The family misses him and wants him to come home."

"Don't give me that garbage, boy. Your parents are the reason that he even came here. Unfortunately, he's no longer here. He left without warning about two days ago, and I don't know where he's gone to. Hey James, for what it's worth coming from me—welcome home."

I nodded my head, turned the horse around, and left.

The road back gave me too much time to think. I needed a quiet place to gather myself and decide what to do next.

I May Never See Him Again

I took Abby to a nearby creek so she could get some water and eat, while I thought about my next move. Right now, I am at a complete loss. It seems like my trail began and ended at the Colston farm. I'm afraid that he may have just completely vanished, and I may never see him again. I decided that I need to get back home and talk with the other siblings to figure something out.

On my way back home, I stopped by the telegraph office to try to get in touch with my beautiful Annie. I'll stop by here tomorrow to see if there has been any response.

When I got home, I saw Mom on the porch, and she looked like she'd been crying. I asked her what was wrong. She said that she misses Patrick and wants him to come home.

I scoffed at her and said, "I don't want to hear it. It is entirely your fault he isn't here right now with all of us. You have only Dad and yourself to blame for this. I've been looking for him the past few days with no luck. Do you know where he may have gone?"

I explained to her that I went to the pastor's house that morning and the Colston farm as well. He explained that Patrick had left just a few days earlier, without warning, and he has no idea where he's at. I told her that I believed him and that I was going out to talk to the sheriff in the morning and check the outskirts of town. Since it hasn't been too long since he left there, I'm thinking that he hasn't gone more than 20–25 miles, if that far.

He Lied

The sheriff was of no help whatsoever. He said the same things that I had already been told. As I was leaving the sheriff's office, I ran into a Colston farmhand. I tried to ask him about Patrick, but he was really aggressive toward me and said, "I don't talk to no Yankee traitor."

I turned around and started to get on my horse and leave, when his wife stopped me. She said, "Mr. Colston has been hiding him and lied to you when you were there yesterday. I overheard a conversation between Patrick and Mr. Colston this morning. Mr. Colston gave Patrick an envelope with a substantial amount of money in it and shook hands. Mr. Colston told Patrick to have safe travels, and then he left. I think that he may have gone to the train station."

I jumped on Abby and took off for the train station. It's about three miles outside of town, and I went as fast as I could to get there quickly. I wasn't going to allow stubbornness and pride to tear our family apart at the seams. I saw too many families destroyed and gone forever—from death on the battlefield and diseases in the camps—to allow our family to die over something that has now become so petty.

It only took about ten minutes or so to get there, and the station was empty on the outside. I ran inside and saw only the station master and the telegraph operator. My stomach turned upside down. I was afraid that I would never see my brother again.

I went up to the train master and asked about my brother. He said, "I haven't seen him but only once since returning home. Tell your parents that me and the missus are looking forward to supper Saturday night."

Now I'm more confused than ever. I can't put my finger on this, and it's driving me crazy. The questions keep adding up. Is someone hiding him? Is he still around town somewhere? Is someone letting him stay with them and simply keeping their mouth shut?

So many questions and no answers. Knowing Patrick, he's more than likely living with someone in secrecy or living in the woods.

I had barely begun to process this web of lies when another blow came from hundreds of miles away.

Annie Shot

The only thing I have heard about Annie was a letter from Dr. Shaw. All it said was:

"Annie was shot while trying to protect a patient in a field hospital in central Tennessee. The one who pulled the trigger was shot and killed. She was shot in the stomach, and thankfully all of her vital organs were missed. Since she was already at the hospital, they were quickly able to stop the internal bleeding. I had her transported home at my request. She arrived here three days ago and is under my direct care. She told me to tell you that she loves you with all her heart and can't wait to see you soon. Don't worry, James. She's going to be alright.

With regards – Dr. S."

I felt my heart stop beating. I feel like this is somehow my fault because I wasn't able to protect her like I promised Tyler at Riverside. I couldn't protect Tyler either. I failed to keep Abigail alive, and now I can't seem to keep my family together as well.

I question my self-worth and value as a man now. What good am I to anybody if I can't do this? I could keep strangers alive on the battlefield, but I can't protect the ones I love the most. Sometimes I wonder if I would've been better off dying at Flintlock Valley. I wish that I had.

Carpetbaggers and Occupation

When I got back home, I tried to talk to Mom and Dad about what I had found out, but they simply refused to listen. Dad spoke up and said:

"Don't worry, son, we'll find Patrick, but at the moment we have bigger problems. Carpetbaggers have come and taken control of most of the government. I heard that a peacekeeping force of Union soldiers is on their way here to maintain order during the reconstruction period. People across the South are rioting and threatening to pick up arms again to get rid of these people."

They were especially hated in the South, and riots broke out often. They turned violent almost every time, and several people always had to go get stitched up. Not only did we have Northerners coming here to take over the government, but they also took over financially as well. They were making lots of money at the expense of Southerners suffering and trying to rebuild their lives, by setting up businesses so they could charge as much as they wanted without anyone saying anything to them.

A company of about 100 Union soldiers arrived this morning and set up camp along the main road near the train station. I found this to be particularly interesting because camps are set up in strategic locations, so if that was the case here, then what's their plan? Whatever it may be, I'm sure it's not going to be a good thing for us. We were told that they're only here as a peacekeeping force and will not disrupt day-to-day activities. They also said that part of their mission is to make sure the newly freed slaves are treated fairly.

I think one of the things that's really upsetting everyone is that they're now taking over the role of law enforcement and have relieved the sheriff of his duties. Personally, I don't think people had a problem with the sheriff being removed, but now you have a Union occupation force taking over the rule of law. I already know where this is heading. Last night there was a clash between some of the former Confederate soldiers and the Union troops. In total, five were killed and around 15–20 wounded combined.

The commander of this occupying force immediately issued martial law. The ringleaders have been arrested and will be charged with the murder of the three Union soldiers killed and the twelve who were injured. They will also be charged with attempted murder of federal soldiers. All carry the death penalty, and since it came down from Washington that all Confederates are classified as rebels, they have no constitutional protection or the right to an attorney. Before the guilty verdicts were handed down, the commander stated, "I will keep martial law in effect and apply other restrictions until you backwoods hillbillies learn to behave." All the men were found guilty of murder and attempted murder and were sentenced to death by hanging. Before the trial had even begun, they were already tying up nooses on two of the giant oak trees just outside the center of town. They hung all ten that afternoon, and it only took about 30 minutes.

The Hell of Sleep

Even though it has now been a few months since the war ended, I still have serious trouble sleeping at night—or at all, for that matter. I still see the faces of the ones I killed and hear the screams of the wounded. Every time I close my eyes, they are there, haunting me like a thousand ghosts and demons, torturing the very depths of my soul. I wake up screaming and covered in sweat. I fear the mere thought of trying to sleep because of the torture that I am about to face.

My depression is at an all-time high, and the thought of suicide has become a constant and reliable companion that I can't get rid of. I find no happiness in anything anymore, and when I look down at my sidearm, all I hear are the voices in my head telling me to go ahead and do it—end my suffering. I feel like I'm in an extremely dark place and don't know how to get out of it. It haunts me in the daytime as well as the night. There are times that I truly just want to pull the trigger and end it altogether so that I can find peace. I pray for death and welcome it with open arms.

As much as I try to live the prewar life that I did, I realize that person died on the battlefield, leaving this shell of who I was behind.

I've become extremely confrontational and quick to anger and fight. The lowest time came when I got angry over something that really didn't matter and hit my dad. I just went outside, saddled my horse, and left. I was so ashamed of myself for that and couldn't look him or her in the eyes anymore. Some of the soldiers have turned to alcohol and drugs like morphine and opium to try to ease the pain—both physical and emotional. I can't say that I haven't thought about using drugs, but I see the effects it is having on some of these guys.

I still haven't heard anything from Annie herself. As a matter of fact, all I've heard is that telegram from Dr. Shaw. Sometimes I wonder if she even loves me anymore. My heart truly aches for her touch. I miss the smile that made my day brighter even in the middle of a battle. Her kisses would just melt away all the worries and trauma I was facing. I hope and pray that she is thinking about me as much as I do her.

Come On, This Is Stupid

With all the new restrictions and martial law that have been placed upon the town, movements have become much more difficult. Martial law takes effect at 8 p.m. and goes till 6 a.m. every day of the week. Being off your property is strictly forbidden, and anyone caught off-property will be either arrested or shot. If you are told to stop and decide to try to run, you will be shot and killed—no exceptions. Any child under the age of fifteen who is caught will be arrested, along with the parents of said child. Anyone over the age of fifteen will be subject to being shot.

Any woman who's about to give birth must request special paperwork from the commanding officer allowing her and her husband to be out after curfew, and the doctor must sign off on the paperwork verifying that she's about to deliver a child. Visual verifications of any kind will not be accepted. Any woman and man caught will be arrested and released upon the doctor verifying the next morning that she's about to give birth.

At any time of day or night, your house is subject to inspection. They say that the purpose of these "inspections" is to make sure people are staying in compliance with the law and that no freed slaves are being held against their will. If any are found, then everyone in that house is arrested and sentenced to prison for kidnapping. The children will either live with a family member or be transported up north to be placed in foster care. I believe these inspections are to see what kind of weapons are in the house and how many. They continually say that they're only here to maintain peace and enforce the changes needed to come back into the Union.

My Search Resumes

I keep a low profile around the soldiers because, even though everyone in town knows I fought for the Union, I don't want them to be aware of that. I'm already having serious problems of my own just getting adapted back to civilian life and not fighting anymore. I really don't need to add that trouble too. I wore the blue uniform to fight against the institution of slavery and all that it represented, but now that the war is over, I'm just a southern man raised in the mountains of north Georgia.

With my search for Patrick continuing, I made sure to leave specific instructions with the station master to contact me if he tries to buy a ticket out of town and to do his best to stall the departure of the train. Now that I have that covered, I am free to search in different areas. With the time restrictions, I have to actually plan my routes. There's only one main road that goes through the center of town, but several that lead out toward different farms.

Found At Last

Several more days have passed, and still no sign of Patrick anywhere. I'm beginning to believe that he has indeed left town and that I may never see him again. I spend time down at the creek thinking about Annie and whether she is okay. I had just dozed off when I heard the sound of a hammer clicking. At first, I thought it was just another nightmare from the war, but then someone kicked my boots. I opened my eyes and saw a pistol pointing at me. Whoever this is has their face covered, so I couldn't tell who it was. Since I fought for the Union during the war, I managed to gather a lot of enemies in town. He pulled down the bandana covering his face and simply said, "I heard you was looking for me." It was my brother Patrick!

I jumped up really quick and ran right into a right hook that put me back on the ground. I was confused as to what had just happened. Then he said that was for the beating I gave him at Flintlock Valley and the pain and suffering he had to endure while at a prisoner-of-war camp in Pennsylvania. He helped me up and gave me a big hug. I squeezed him really hard and put us both in the creek. We wrestled around for a few minutes, laughing like two kids. After we got out of the water, we laid on the ground and talked for hours. I was so happy that I finally found him—or, well, that he found me.

But joy, like all things since the war, never lasted long.

I told him that I wanted him to come home so we could mend the family and not let it stay torn apart. He said, "Mom and Dad have already made it very clear that I am not welcome at their house anymore and to never darken their door again. I've been living in the woods." I asked him how he had been surviving. He smiled and said to me, "I've been stealing from the Union camp."

She's Dying

I told him that it was time to go home now. He argued with me for a few minutes, but eventually agreed to go try it one more time. We got on our horses and were heading home when I was met by a dispatcher. "I was told to get this to you as quick as possible." I hadn't even opened it or looked to see who it was from, but I knew it was about Annie. The telegram read:

"Dear James, Annie's condition has taken a turn for the worse. She's developed a bad infection from a fragment of the bullet that is still inside her that I wasn't able to remove. I've been doing my best to get rid of the infection, but only with limited success. She has not responded to anything or anyone for the past 24 hours. I would suggest that you get up here as soon as you possibly can. You will find a $50 bank transfer I sent to you to help cover the cost of travel and food. Please hurry. — Dr. S."

I broke down in tears at the thought that the love of my life could be dead by the time I got there to her.

Patrick told me that I was in no condition to go alone. He said, "Let's wait till we return to let them know that we found each other." We quickly rode home, and with Patrick outside, I ran into the house and explained the situation as I was grabbing clothes. The two of us quickly rode to the train station. We had to wait for about an hour for the train to arrive, and that was truly the longest hour of my life. While I was there, I sent Dr. Shaw a telegram saying that I was on the next train. We traveled almost all the way by train and then the rest on horseback.

When we finally arrived, she was near death, barely breathing and not moving a single muscle. He told me that she hadn't responded to his voice in a few days now, and he was afraid that she wouldn't come out of this. I couldn't stop crying and was angry, because once again it seemed like someone I love was going to die from the war.

I finally regained some composure and went into the room. I leaned over and gave her a kiss and told her I was here and I loved her. She tried to open her eyes, so I called the doctor in. He was excited and confused at the same time. Once again, I called her name and said it was me, and this time she opened her eyes all the way. She smiled and said in a soft and weak voice, "My lover, is it really you?" I told her yes, it's really me. She put her hand on my face and said that she loved me, then closed her eyes again and fell back asleep.

He informed me that when he finally found the remaining piece, he had to remove a small part of her stomach to make sure he got all of it. As of right now, he doesn't know if she's going to live or die. Her aunt and uncle put us up in one of the hotel rooms free of charge, so I could focus on her. To earn our keep, Patrick and I have been doing maintenance on the house. Even though I didn't grow up here, it's still really tough for me to be here. I can't imagine the pain that Annie—and for that matter, the whole family—is going through.

We were happy to help clean up and do some repairs for them. Since Larry can't help and Tyler is dead, it got run down really quickly. As I stand here in the house where my best friend lived, I can't hold back the tears. And with the woman I want to marry down the road fighting for her life, it becomes more than I can handle at the moment. Patrick runs over and catches me just before I fall, takes me outside, and tells me to get away from here for a while. So, I went and got Larry, and the two of us went for a long ride.

I was really concerned about Patrick coming with me. Mainly because he fought for the Confederacy, I didn't know how he would be received by her family—not to mention all the Union soldiers around everywhere. We had a long talk on the way up there, and I explained to him that I do understand his anger and hatred toward the soldiers, but that he must control his temper. I also explained that under no circumstances is he to try and provoke any of them. With all the former Confederate soldiers trying to reignite the war, he could be taken prisoner for something he has no part in. He agreed and said that he was there for me and not to cause any trouble. I was really happy to hear that, because I hadn't met any of these people in person. When we finally got there, we were greeted with open arms.

I'm spending most of my time with Annie at the hospital. Since our arrival, she has become more aware and is now trying to talk. She still sleeps most of the day, but that's expected for now. There's a nurse who comes in several times a day to help keep her clean, and I do appreciate all that they do for her.

I was happy to hear that Larry gave Patrick permission to stay at the Barrett farm while he fixes it up to sell. I don't go there to see him often, because I can't handle the pain associated with that house. Patrick told me that he has found solace and peace living there. It's given him a way to channel all the nightmares he's been having. He's got the place fixed up really nicely now. The windows that were broken have been fixed, the stovepipe has been repaired, and the leaks in the ceiling have been fixed. He also replaced all the flooring, so it looks like a brand-new house. Larry, Debby, and I went out there to see it, and they were most pleased.

We've been up here for a few weeks now, and I finally got the chance to contact Mom and Dad. I told them that Annie is making progress and that Dr. Shaw told me she may survive this. When he found the last piece of the bullet, he had to also remove a piece of her stomach to make sure no infection sets in and kills her. I also told them that I found Patrick and he is here with me. When she gets better, the three of us are coming home, and all of us are going to sit down and straighten this nonsense out.

Ready to Leave the Hospital

After a month in the hospital, Annie has recovered quite well. Over the past week, she's been up walking and able to eat more than soups. Dr. Shaw told me that he is planning on letting her leave in a couple more days. She's still weak, but she is probably one of the toughest women I've ever met. She has said to me several times that I rescued her, but in actuality, I believe that she rescued me instead. I don't know of very many women who could handle what she's handled—physically and mentally—over the past few years and still have enough heart left to love someone like me.

Dr. Shaw feels that she's well enough to come home now, but he wants to check on her once a week to make sure the infection doesn't try to return. She was adamant about not staying at the old homeplace because the pain would be too much to bear. I explained to her that I fully understand, and every time I go to see or help Patrick, I can't stay long. She was happy that Patrick is staying there fixing up the place. I explained everything he's done to it, and she smiled and said she would thank him next time she sees him. She wants to sell the place once all the repairs are made.

It is now October, and the weather is starting to get colder. Annie, Patrick, and I sat down and agreed to stay here for the winter and get all the affairs settled so in spring we can leave. We got the stable sold pretty quickly and have had several people interested in the house, but no buyers yet. We both agreed to sign the rights to the hotel and the restaurant next to the hotel over to her aunt Debby and uncle Larry, with Annie receiving 25% of the profits monthly. That may not sound like a whole lot, but it will help when we get married (that is, when I stop being such a chicken).

Her family has been wonderful toward us and even call us family. I'm really proud of the self-restraint that Patrick has shown lately. Since he has a real deep Southern accent, people have mocked him and called him some very nasty names. Just a few years ago, he would have jumped them and fought them, but now he just sits back and smiles at them. I'm glad too, because if he got into a fight I would have to join in and help him, and I really don't want to do that. I'm sick of any type of violence. I just want to live the rest of my life in peace.

The war has changed everyone involved, and the mental damage isn't quite so obvious. Some people have returned to their prewar life relatively easily, while many are hopelessly addicted to drugs and alcohol to try to drown out the nightmares and the screams. Yet there are others who have turned to a life of crime because they're addicted to a different drug—the drug of violence. Some people can't let go of the feeling of taking a life or creating absolute fear. These men are extremely violent and very unpredictable. These people are easy to recognize because they travel in groups—sometimes as many as ten. When they walk into a bar, people don't talk to or mess with them. The only outcome is you getting put into a pine box.

Annie is no exception to this. What little sleep she gets now is plagued with the screams of the wounded getting limbs cut off, and the death and destruction on the battlefield. She cries almost every night from the nightmares, and I feel so helpless. We do, at times, talk about what happened, but it's a very slow healing process. She tries to show a strong face because she wants me to think that she's okay, but I know differently. I told her once that I truly believe the only way to get true peace will be when death comes.

I want to tell her about Abigail, but I'm kind of afraid to. Annie is a bit of the jealous type, so I'm afraid of how she'll interpret my intentions and take everything the wrong way. If she sees another woman talking to me and getting even a little flirty, she tells them to leave and never talk to me again—or else. Telling her about what they did to Abigail and her family, and how I killed them, will be extremely easy. But explaining the rest of it—that won't be so easy for her to understand.

My heart has always been, and always belonged, to Annie, but my conscience is eating me alive, and she knows this is different from everything else. She keeps asking me to tell her, but I just keep saying that I'm alright. Annie is a very smart and instinctive woman, so she won't let me keep this curtain up for long. Patrick and I sat and talked about the whole situation, including the kiss, telling her that I loved Abigail, and how I sat there and cried over her. All he said was, "Tread lightly on broken glass—you might get cut."

And yet, even while drowning in personal demons, the world outside wasn't getting any kinder.

Time to Tell Her

I need to tell her so my conscience can rest, but I haven't found the right time. I'm starting to think there will be no right time, so I guess I'll just have to say it and pray she doesn't leave me over this.

She looked up at me with those soft, loving eyes of hers and all but begged me to tell her. I said, "Let's go get supper, and I will tell you everything. I need you to completely listen and try to understand." So, with her promise, I proceeded to tell her about the three Confederates, finding Abigail and what they had done to her and her family. How we found them, and that I had killed them, and how she begged me to take her with me—and even though I didn't like the idea, I reluctantly agreed.

By this point, Annie was in tears. I told her about the kiss and how I pulled back and said that my heart belongs to someone else—someone I am trying to get home to. I was surprised that she wasn't that upset about it. She said, "I don't blame her for kissing you. I probably would've tried to do more." I was in tears when I told her how Abigail died, and I feel a little guilty for not being able to save her. Annie leaned over and gave me a soft kiss and said, "At that moment, she needed you—and you did save her. Even though she died from the wounds they caused, you gave her peace knowing the monsters who did this are now dead. I am so proud of you, and I love you for what you did." I told her that I was so nervous about telling her the kiss part, and that's how the horse got the name Abby—because it belonged to her, and I felt it was appropriate to do that.

Even as life settled into something resembling peace, healing wasn't so simple—for any of us.

Winters here in Ohio are a lot colder than the ones we have in the South. Don't get me wrong, winter gets cold there too, but not nearly as much snow, sleet, and freezing rain. We do get snow, but not all the time like it is here. I'm over it. It's almost Christmas now, and Annie still can't stay at the family home for long, so we all agreed to have it at the restaurant instead. We popped popcorn and made garlands with it; it took twice as long because little Miss Annie couldn't keep her sticky fingers out of it. Patrick and I went and cut down a tree, and we all decorated it with popcorn garlands all over. After lunch, we closed the restaurant, and the women went to cooking for our Christmas supper—and what a meal it was. They cooked turkey, corn, green beans, cornbread, with apple and cherry pies for dessert. There were only supposed to be five people, but Annie and Debby cooked for an entire army.

Emily

We had all been noticing how Patrick had been abnormally happy these past few weeks, but he would never tell us why. Well, we found out: her name is Emily. She's short like Annie, with really dark hair and brown eyes. Annie and Emily looked at each other like they had both just seen a ghost. They both squealed and ran into each other's arms. Come to find out, they had grown up together. When Emily was about ten, her parents moved away and they lost contact. So, to say they were happy to see each other would be an understatement. The evening was filled with laughter.

There was sadness in the air as well. At one point, Annie became quite distraught and left the table for some fresh air. I gave her a few minutes, then I went outside to check on her. She cried on my shoulder and said, "My family is dead now. I have no mother or father to talk to or confide in anymore." I reminded her that she still had me and her

Aunt Debby. She looked up at me, smiled, and said, "You are right. I was just being silly." We saw Dr. Shaw and convinced him to join us as well. It was a wonderful night for everyone.

From Sadness to Joy

Annie was still having a really rough time, though. This was the first Christmas at home without her parents. She would vanish for long stretches to go cry. She would try to tell me that she hadn't been crying, but her eyes told a different story. She broke down and told me, "Oh James, I feel so lost. Mom and Dad are dead, I'm the only living child—I truly feel like an orphan now." I told her, "I made your dad a promise at the Battle of Riverside. He asked me to take care of you if he died. So, I'm going to fulfill that promise. Annabelle Grace Barrett, will you do me the honor of becoming Mrs. James Calloway and forever be mine?" She jumped into my arms and screamed, "Yes, yes, a million times yes!"

Everyone heard the commotion outside and came running out to see what all the fuss was about. She ran over to Emily, saying, "I'm about to become Mrs. James Calloway." Everyone was congratulating us when I noticed Dr. Shaw walking back toward his office. I ran after him, and when I caught up, I asked him what was the matter.

"James, I truly am happy for the both of you. She deserves a good man like you. Over the years, I've developed a real fondness for her, and I do admit that I have romantic feelings for her. But I will assure you under oath that I will never think about acting on them. I see how she looks at you and how her eyes light up in your presence. I know that she has true love for you, and I would never try to interfere with that. I pray that you allow us to remain friends, but if you say no, then no it is."

I was quite confused and asked him what he was trying to tell me.

"Did she tell you my plans? I was going to take her under my wing and make her my full-time assistant—and eventually let her run this office completely."

Stunned, I said, "Oh my—she never mentioned this to me at all. I had no idea." He patted me on the shoulder and walked away.

I stood there, surprised and shocked as to why she would never mention such a great opportunity—for her and for us—and why she would throw away her dreams like this. I understand that living here would be a serious emotional challenge for her, but this is her dream we're talking about.

She walked out just as Shaw was patting me on the shoulder and came over to make sure everything was okay. I asked her why she didn't tell me about Dr. Shaw's plan to make her his assistant and eventually take over his office.

"Do you not realize what an honor this would be? And how this could change the course of history for women and medicine?"

She said in a stern voice, "James, becoming your wife and the mother of your children is the most important thing to me in this world, and nobody is going to stop that, mister—do you understand me? I will go talk to Dr. Shaw, I promise."

I smirked, gave her a soft kiss, and said, "That's the little fireball I've been missing lately. I love you, Mrs. Calloway."

The Conversation with Dr Shaw

That next morning, Annie went to talk to Dr. Shaw. She told me this later that night.

"When I walked into his office, he seemed cold and distant toward me. When I asked him what was wrong, in a concerned voice, he just replied, 'Nothing.' I said, 'Wait, you're upset because James and I are getting married.' He turned and said, before he caught himself, 'Yes, Annie, I love you and…' he stopped, and this really confused me for a moment. 'Listen, I am happy for the two of you, I really am, but I guess I was hoping that we would get married one day and start our own family.'

'Oh, Stanley, why are you telling me this now?'

'I wanted you to know before you left that I love you very much and always will.'

As I was walking out of his office, he turned me around and kissed me and groped me. I kneed him in the groin and ran out of his office as quickly as I could. I was scared that James had seen me, and I knew he would kill him. So, I didn't want to tell him about it. When I did tell him, all he said to me was, 'I didn't want her alone with him again,' and I agreed with him."

The relationship between Patrick and Emily seems to be taking off really well. He said that she's been talking about a possible double wedding. When he said that, we both looked at each other and said, "Absolutely not." He said that he hasn't even proposed yet, and that seems to be all she wants to talk about. I've noticed that her presence has helped him begin the journey of moving on from the battlefield to home, just as Annie has helped me—and I help her too.

I wrote back home and everyone is excited about our engagement and happy for Patrick as well. Annie really wanted to have the wedding back at my home, and I told her that I thought that was a great idea. It's now coming up on springtime, and we're starting to make preparations for the move back to Georgia. The hotel and restaurant have been completely turned over to Uncle Larry and Aunt Debby. The house and land were purchased by Mr. Whitley, and for the moment, he's letting Patrick live there rent-free in honor of his service. Emily has told her parents that she's moved into the hotel to be close to Annie, but she has actually moved in with Patrick.

She Feels So Helpless

Emily has been a great help to Patrick and a godsend in his recovery. She's been there to help pick him up when he's on the floor having a nightmare. She holds him in his sleep when he starts crying. She truly is a wonderful woman, and I do believe that she loves him deeply. I'm thankful that she has come into his life—I know he is.

I overheard a conversation between her and Annie. Emily asked, with tears in her eyes, "How do I heal the mental wounds that Patrick has suffered? I feel so helpless, and I truly love him and I'm not going anywhere, but I don't know how to help him. Sometimes, we will be having a conversation and he will just start staring off into space. I have to yell his name several times to bring him back to me. Annie, I feel so terrible when I have to yell because he is so good to me, and I feel like a bad person when I do. When he does that, I dare not touch him. I accidentally did that one night and when he came to himself, we were on the floor with him on top of me, and the look in his eyes was more terrifying than the thought of getting hit. When he realized what was going on, he laid on top of me and cried and begged for forgiveness. So, my beloved sister, what do I do and how do you handle James?"

"Emily, the situation between James and myself is completely different than that between you and Patrick. Since we both fought in the war from different perspectives, we understand the difficulties. Honey, there have been many nights that I lay there crying from a nightmare, or James will find me on the floor trying to amputate a limb, or yelling for assistance holding someone down. When that happens, he sits down beside me and when I come to, he just holds me until I stop crying. I guess all I can tell you is don't try to heal him—he has to do that on his own. But be there to hold him. Emily, I will tell you this: you know I love you like a sister, but if you don't plan on being with him for the rest of your life, leave him now. If I find out that you're just playing head games with him, you won't need to worry about his sister or mother—I will kill you myself. Understand? These boys have been through enough. You better make it soon, too."

Annie gave her a big hug and told her that she loved her, but meant everything she said. She walked away, leaving Emily standing there crying. I went over to make sure she was alright. She said she was, but I know how brutally honest Annie can get. That's why I call her my little fireball. She can be very passionate when it comes to the ones she loves.

You Got to Be Kidding

We're now just a few days away from beginning our journey back to Georgia when Patrick comes running up to Annie and me in a panic. After a few minutes, he calms down enough to say, "She… she's… pregnant! I'm going to be a daddy." Having said the words out loud, it hit him what was happening. All I could get out was, "How did this happen?" Patrick and Annie gave me this "you got to be kidding" look and at the same time said, "Seriously?" So now we have to come up with another plan, and Annie quickly pointed out that the risk of losing the baby was too great to take the chance.

As soon as she told him, he immediately proposed to her, and of course she said yes. Now, her parents weren't fond of him in the least—mainly because he fought for the Confederacy. He was used to the name-calling and harassment, so that didn't bother him. Emily said that she already told her parents that she was pregnant, and her dad started screaming and throwing things. Then she said that he wants to talk to Patrick. Her family owns several hundred acres and has several hundred cattle that he sells and makes really good money from. He's a third-generation cattle rancher, so he's used to being able to intimidate.

You Are Not Going Alone

I told all three that I was going with him to talk to Mr. Stockton. There was no way I was going to let him go up there alone. Patrick agreed to go unarmed, but I was armed to the teeth in case any of his farmhands decided to get stupid. I carried two .45 caliber pistols on my sides, another .38 caliber above my right ankle, and a knife on my back. I was ready to fight if need be.

When we arrived, the farmhand at the gate said that only Patrick was allowed in. Then, when he went to reach for the stirrups of my horse, he heard the sound of a pistol cocking. I explained to him that either he lets go of my horse or he dies—his choice.

He then opened the gate, and the two of us proceeded toward the house. The house itself was just a plain white two-story house on the outside. There were trees lining each side of the driveway leading to the house and lots of different types of flowers. The barn sat off to the left of the house and was bigger than the house itself. Of course, the stable was on the bottom, and just outside of it was the pen where they train and keep their horses. The loft was open and had so much hay up there I bet it would last several years. On the left side of the house sat a field of at least five acres and had several different types of vegetables.

We were escorted into the house by two armed guards. I was asked to relinquish my pistol belt. I told them that I wasn't there to cause any trouble—I was only there to make sure that my brother walked out of there safely. I also told them that I would be happy to take off my pistol belt when they put down their rifles. Just as things were beginning to get really heated, this monster of a man with a deep voice came in and said, "Gentlemen, gentlemen, calm down. Is this any way to treat our future family with such disrespect?" I don't know who was more confused—Patrick, myself, or the guards.

His office was quite huge as well. It looked to be at least 30 feet long and about 20 feet wide, with two doors opposite each other. There were two windows on each side. His desk sat close to the door in the back of the room—either for intimidation or escape, or possibly both. Under his desk was a rug that he clearly got from the Orient. It had different types of birds on it and was gorgeous. There were also two chairs sitting at the front of his desk for visitors. One of the guards positioned himself near the desk so that if Patrick tried something, he would be shot before he got close. I was standing between the two windows, watching everyone's movements. The other guard was on the other side with his gun pointed toward me.

The Conversation

As expected, he tried to buy Patrick off, but my brother stood his ground. This went on for about 10 minutes or so. When Patrick quickly turned down $30,000, Mr. Stockton knew then that he wasn't going to be bought. That statement Mr. Stockton made when he came into the room is still ringing in my ears, and I'm on my guard. Did he mean it, or did he say it to try to gain the upper hand?

At one point, I looked at the guard standing to my left and said in a stern voice, "I have already explained to you that I am not here to cause trouble. I am just here to make sure that my brother leaves here alive. I would greatly appreciate it if you would stop pointing that rifle at me—it's making me nervous. It's clear we are outgunned, and I am not stupid." Mr. Stockton chuckled and motioned to the guards to lower their weapons.

My gut is still telling me that something is up. I am not sure if it's my own paranoia, the fact that we could easily be gunned down, or if Stockton is being sincere. Patrick has made his intentions perfectly clear about marrying Emily and standing by her side. Stockton is trying to bully him into giving in and staying there after they're married, making him one of his senior farmhands. They would have their own space and the children their own room. Stockton said he would pay Patrick $20 a day, whereas the normal starting pay is $7 a day. Patrick concluded that he must talk about this with Emily. Both Patrick and Stockton stood up, shook hands, and exchanged a few pleasantries. Then Stockton looked over at me and said, "You are a good brother, and I would hate to cross you on a bad day." I smiled, and then the two of us walked out. Until we left the Stockton property, I kept my hand on my pistols at all times.

We later met up with Annie and Emily to discuss a new plan since Patrick and Emily literally screwed this one up. If we wait until she's safe to travel, then we're looking at September or October. If we leave now as planned, the chance of a miscarriage is high, and she could also die. Annie still will not go and talk to Shaw since the assault, so I told her I would go if she gave me a list of what is needed. She told me she would give it to her uncle Larry, because if she gave it to me or Patrick to get, then I would have to bail you out of jail.

The Patrick–Emily Wedding

They wanted us to go ahead as planned and leave, but wanted to postpone until after the wedding so I could be best man and she could be maid of honor. We both agreed and decided to stay an extra two weeks. I've spent a lot of time hanging out with Patrick lately since the women have been busy planning this wedding. They decided to get married at the house. I thought it wasn't a good idea, but it's not my wedding. Emily said that her parents would have wanted that. Her daddy said it was to be there, and "no" wasn't an option.

I must admit that I am proud of how he has stepped up and taken full responsibility for his actions. The prewar Patrick would have never done that. He was always one to cause a problem and then blame someone else. It was always someone else's fault for his actions. So to see this from my brother is really a good thing, and I am proud of him. I told Emily how much he has grown up, and that a few years ago he would've been on the first stage out, but now he's standing up, taking all the responsibility. I said, "Emily, I am proud to call you my sister, and you bring honor to the Calloway name."

The wedding was a beautiful one. Seeing Annie in that green dress with flowers on it and the headpiece made out of daisies was absolutely breathtaking. I know that this was their wedding, but I so wanted to jump up there and make it a double wedding. But Annie said she wanted to get married back at my home. It was an indoor wedding since the ground was wet from the recent rains. It was in the formal room of the house. There were two small candelabras on each side with two candles each and a bigger third one in the middle with five candles on it. There were flowers around the windows and a musician playing a harp in the corner of the room. The rest of the house was decorated with different types of floral arrangements and had two candelabras in each room. In each corner of the main room stood individual ones about seven feet tall, each with a single candle. Emily was absolutely gorgeous. She wore a white dress with a headpiece made from yellow roses and a white veil. I looked at Patrick, and he had tears in his eyes. I must admit I did too when I saw my Annie.

They wrote their own vows. Emily went first:

"Patrick, from the first moment I saw you, I knew you were mine. I never knew that love existed on this level. My love for you is a never-ending fountain straight from our Heavenly Father into my soul. You make me smile and my heart jump just being in your sight. I will always love, cherish, and honor you till my dying breath."

Patrick: "My beloved Emily, the one and only star in the night sky directing my paths when I can't see. I know that I'm not easy to deal with because of the haunting of my war years, but you're always my refuge, and even when I'm at my lowest, you're there at your strongest. Just being around you has brought me so much joy and peace, it's truly difficult to put into words. I promise to love, cherish, and honor you till my dying breath."

Due to the number of people that came, the reception was held in the barn, where there was a lot more open room. As I always do, I was standing in the corner by myself, just enjoying the men on stage playing the guitars. Annie tried to get me to go dance, but I don't dance, so I was enjoying watching her. No matter what, she was always looking at me, and every time a new song played, she would ask if she could stay on the floor—and of course, I didn't stop her. One thing that made me proud was that if they played a slower song, she refused to dance with another man. Just watching her was like watching an angel—it stole my heart again.

Stockton's Offer

After a little while, Mr. Stockton came over to talk.

"So, James, I hope that you're enjoying yourself."

"Yes, I am, and Annie is too."

"I heard that you fought with Tyler. He was a great man."

"Yes sir, he truly was my best friend, and my heart is still sad about his passing. We saved each other's lives several times. I just couldn't get there to him fast enough to save him. But he was one hell of a soldier. The day he died, he was fighting five men at one time. He managed to kill three before the other two got behind him and stabbed him with their bayonets several times. Even then, he didn't go down easy. I made sure that the stretcher bearers got him to the field hospital in time to say goodbye to Annie."

"I am truly sorry to hear about that, but let's move on to a different matter. You know that I offered Patrick that top hand position, but for some reason he hasn't responded to me about it."

"I've asked him as well, and he isn't saying much. I know that he's torn right now. See, Mr. Stockton, our family was absolutely against slavery and often—quite often—spoke out against it. Needless to say, when Patrick left to fight for the South, it literally tore our house in half. He was banished from the family, and when he came home, my parents and siblings refused to even talk to him. I have made peace between them, and I know he wants to move back to Georgia. When I talked to Emily about it, all she said was that she wanted to stay here but would follow her husband."

"I actually came over to talk to you. I have two positions opening up that I think you would be great for. The first one is putting you in charge of the cattle and everything that it entails. That means moving the cattle from here to the railroad, about 25 miles away. Making sure that they are fed every day and maintaining discipline among the cowboys while at the markets. Each one has several brothels, and I don't allow my men to go in until the sale is done and they're paid. They also know better than to mistreat the women, so if that happens, I want them brought back tied up, and I will take care of them. You will receive $40 a week while here and $500 once the sale is complete. If you take this position, don't discuss pay or let anyone else either. I pay differently for each man."

The next one is the one that I really hope you take. I need a new head of security. The way you handled yourself and how you put that guard in his place really impressed me. Your assignment will be the protection of myself and my family. Part of your duties will include managing the schedules of the guards, and I will let you handle the hiring and firing of guards—all I ask is that you talk to me first about it. Most of the time, wherever I go, I will have four guards plus you. Now, I haven't had a problem, and I don't expect any, but a person can never be too cautious. This one keeps you here unless I am traveling and pays $50 a week, and $75 a week when traveling, plus an additional $10 a day for trips into town. Both options allow you to stay in the house or in the guest house at no charge."

"Wow, Mr. Stockton, I really appreciate these offers, but as you are aware, I will need to discuss all this with Annie. I'll have an answer for you in two days, and I'll make sure that Patrick does too."

"That would be wonderful. Enjoy the rest of your evening, James."

Now Where Did He Go

My first task will be getting Patrick to respond. I don't know why it's taking so long, but I am going to find out. I went to talk to Emily, and she said he hasn't been home in a couple of days. After getting on to her about not saying anything, I went to find him again.

I talked to one of the lead field hands and told him that sometimes, due to the depression and not being able to sleep at night because of the nightmares, Patrick will wander off for a day or so, then come back. He does it to clear his head and refocus on the things he needs to do. I got his word that he won't tell anyone—especially Mr. Stockton. If that ever becomes an issue, then I will.

It didn't take me too long to find him. He was asleep under a tree, drunk. I worry about him and his drinking because it is too easy to try to use drugs and/or alcohol to drown out the pain and anguish of losing the war and all the suffering that comes with it.

Life Has Become Hell

I've been in contact with Mom and Dad, and they've been saying that things have gotten bad.

"The carpetbaggers have taken control of most of the governments in the South, and the states have been placed under military jurisdictions commanded by Northern generals. Something known as the 'new social order' has taken effect, and it's made enough people mad across the South that the threat of another civil war has become a real possibility.

Sharecropping and tenant farming have replaced slavery and plantation farming and now use contract labor. Most of the freed slaves have stayed on, knowing now that they'll be paid for their labor, which is something your father and I agree with. Even though the war is over and slaves have been freed, most are still being treated as such. Something known as 'black codes' has been placed on most Blacks, and though it's illegal now, it's used to restrict activity and the movements of freedmen to ensure availability for forced labor.

Racial segregation is still bad—freed Blacks are given really low-paying and most dangerous jobs. Your father and I are thinking about leaving the South altogether and heading west.

This so-called Reconstruction has severely limited the rights of former Confederate soldiers. Some have even lost their citizenship. Most of the former soldiers have refused to accept the terms of the new social order and have been charged and prosecuted for participation in the war. I heard that most of the politicians have fled to Europe and Mexico to escape prosecution. Jeff Davis has been arrested and is facing trial for his role. Former soldiers are severely limited in their ability to run for office of any kind. All soldiers have been stripped of their status as war veterans, so they're not able to get any federal help in their recovery.

It seems that the only help some of these soldiers are getting is from drugs and alcohol. The suicide rates are really high—up to 50 a day are killing themselves, mostly because of the nightmares and shame of losing the war. It seems like almost every day there are clashes between former Confederates and Union occupiers. Thankfully, we've been able to grow our own food, because food is scarce, and your father and I have been giving away most of what we grow and can to our neighbors to make sure they have food to eat.

Don't worry about us. Take care of Annie, and we can't wait to meet her—and Emily too.

With all my love,

Mom."

After waking Patrick up, I read him the letter I had just received from Mom, and he just sat there and wept. I also asked him why he was refusing to give Mr. Stockton an answer. He told me that Emily said it's a good idea, but his heart is still back home. I reminded him of what's going on and told him I understand how he feels, but I believe it's in his best interest, for the time being, to wait before going home.

I explained the conversation that Stockton and I had at his wedding reception, and while I'm not sure because I haven't discussed this with Annie yet, I plan to tonight—because I promised Stockton that he would get both answers by tomorrow.

At supper that night, I explained that Stockton wanted me to take over as head of security for him and his family and that the pay would be $50 a week while at home, $75 a week while traveling, and an additional $10 per day for going into town. He also said we would be living rent-free, either in the main house or in the guest house.

The guest house isn't too bad either. It's a three-bedroom cottage with a good-sized kitchen and a connecting outhouse. The porch goes all the way around, and the sitting area is 25x25. The house itself is about 25x100, so there's plenty of room. It's made from brick and mortar, so it's quite warm.

I told her that Patrick accepted the job offer from Mr. Stockton, and I told him I'd have an answer in the morning after we discussed it.

She had one concern, and that was—what about our plans to move back to Georgia? I read her the note Mom sent me and told her that I'm not so sure it would be a good idea at the moment. She said that whatever decision I make, she knows it's in our best interest, and that my word is final. She'll support whatever I decide to do.

I know she has her heart set on getting married back in my hometown, and I told her, "I know you want a Southern wedding, and we will go ahead with our original plans and see what the situation is really like back home. You'll learn quickly that Mom can—and does—stretch the truth some." Her eyes lit up and she gave me a big kiss.

I know she really wants to leave here, and I get that. But I can't fully understand how she truly feels and the silent pain she's going through right now. I just need to make sure that I'm there for her, as she is for me.

I went and sat down with Mr. Stockton to talk about what we had decided, and he told me he understood but was disappointed that I didn't accept the position. I told him that I really needed to see the situation for myself, and that Annie really wanted to get married in my hometown and get away from here.

He said he would hold off for two months on hiring someone else, just in case I changed my mind. I told him I appreciated what he has done for Patrick and that I understand Patrick is still suffering from the war as well.

So, like I explained to Emily when they first met—when he's going through these emotions, just be there and let him work through it. It will work itself out.

Heading Back to Georgia

We spent the next couple of days finalizing the list of things we were taking with us to Georgia and getting it loaded. I was excited to go back home and for Annie to meet my family.

She told me last night that "she's excited to get there and to leave this place behind." She asked if she could go tell Dr. Shaw goodbye and that she forgives him.

I told her that would be a great idea, but I was coming with her—just in case he decided to get stupid. She smiled, and we headed over to his office.

I was extremely apprehensive about this, but she needed to do it so she could have complete closure, so I agreed.

When we got there, he was quite afraid to see me. The funny part was that he ran behind his desk. I couldn't help but chuckle a little bit. Annie made sure that I was calm before we left our room to go see him. I told him that I knew about what he did and that I had promised my fiancé that I wouldn't kill or hurt him. So, I'm just here to make sure you don't try anything like that again.

"I will forever be grateful for all that you taught me and for pushing me to be a better person and nurse. I truly wish the best for you, but I can no longer stand to look at your face. You hurt me badly, emotionally, and I always looked up to you. So, this is goodbye, and I wanted you to know that even though you did that to me, I still forgive you."

With tears in her eyes, we walked out and never looked back.

We went back and loaded everything we could and decided to start the journey early in the morning so we could get as far as possible on that first day. We figured that it would take a day or so to get to the train station, then a day to get to Chattanooga, then unload and go the rest of the way by buggy. I don't expect any trouble, but if what my mom said is true, then we may decide to head west earlier than expected.

The Goodman Gang

Everything went smoothly until we got to Chattanooga. A tree had fallen across the track, and we had to stop to remove it—but it was a trap. Bandits quickly boarded the train and took control of the engineers. They shot one man who stood up and killed him. I knew then that this wasn't going to be a grab-and-go situation.

Before they got to our car, a fellow soldier who sat across from us and I came up with a quick plan. We heard what seemed to be four distinct voices, but we weren't sure that was all of them. I gave Annie a knife and reminded her where to stab, like I had shown her: go between the 2nd and 3rd ribs, puncturing the lung—he won't be able to scream—then put the knife into his throat. That will take his life, but only if he comes to you, and not before.

It didn't take long for them to reach our car. There were just two of them, and as soon as they entered, they started shooting into the air. What they didn't do was count the number of bullets they fired. But Brandon, the one across from me, and I did. Now knowing that their pistols were empty, we let them both pass by us and then jumped them. We wrestled around until another guy walked in and fired a round that barely missed the two of us.

What he didn't take into consideration was my little fireball, who was now very mad because he had taken a shot at her husband. She let him pass by, stood up behind him, and with all her might, stabbed him several times. When he fell down, she stabbed him in the throat. The whole time, she was yelling at him for taking a shot at me and the other man. She stood there shaking, and I went over, took the knife, and gave her a big hug as the entire train car clapped.

But that wasn't the end of the situation. We still had no idea how many more there were or if the engineers were even still alive. We lowered one of the windows to take a quick peek and get an idea of what we were facing. We saw just one more man standing near the engine, but he wasn't paying much attention to what was going on. I think he was so confident in the fear they'd created that he believed nobody would fight back.

I grabbed my pistol and my knife and headed toward the front of the train. Brandon stayed behind to make sure our prisoners remained secured.

When I got to the front near where he was standing, he wasn't even looking around. In fact, he looked like he was sleepy. I stood there for a minute, just looking at the brazen arrogance of this man. He finally turned around and saw me, but it was too late. When he realized I wasn't one of them, he already had a knife in his chest. With several more stabs, he fell over, dead.

I ran up to the front of the engine, and thankfully the engineers weren't hurt—just tied up. They confirmed that there were only four men. We told them that two were dead and two captured. We got the tree moved and were soon back underway.

A few miles up the track, there was a telegraph station and a watering spot for the train. The engineer contacted the local sheriff and told him about the situation. He quickly gathered a posse and came to get the robbers.

He said, "This is—or was now—the Goodman Gang, and we've been trying to find them for over a year. They've been terrorizing trains up and down this railway, and there will be a substantial reward from the owner of this line for this."

We departed the train from there and headed by wagon the remaining 20 or so miles to the house. After several miles, it began to get dark, and we decided to stay and camp for the night, then go the rest of the way in the morning. We should arrive the next day by late evening or so.

Annie told me she wasn't nervous, but I knew that she was. I could hear it in her voice as well as her laughter. Neither of us slept well that night. That morning, we had some salted pork and coffee and hit the road for the last part of this journey home.

The weather was perfect, so we made really good time. We arrived at the house late in the evening and decided to surprise them the next morning. We stayed at a hotel that night and talked and played card games most of the evening. Her favorite was poker, and she was very good at it. To be honest, I think she was too good at it. She beat me most of the time, and I wasn't just letting her win either. All she would say was, "Beginners' luck." I really didn't believe her, but I enjoyed losing to her.

Surprise!!

The next morning came, and we knocked on the door, but nobody answered. I didn't understand what was going on, so I drew my pistol and slowly entered the house. I told Annie to wait by the door, and if she heard any gunshots, to run and get help. I heard some giggling from the main room and saw that the entire family was going to surprise us.

I went back to the door and told Annie what was going on. We decided to turn the tables. We went to the back of the house and came in that way, and when we got behind them, we yelled "Surprise!" and they all jumped. The perfect way to get home.

Everyone was happy to see us, and it wasn't just the family there. The reverend, some of our dear friends, and even Mr. Colston were there. My biggest question was: how did they know when we had arrived, since we didn't tell anyone the exact time?

Then Patrick came out and said, "Surprise, brother. We were on the train that left right after the two of you did. When I heard about the robbery, I was absolutely livid—but I wasn't worried about you two." He said he was more concerned about Emily than anything else because of her condition. He said she made it fine and was upstairs resting. The next thing I knew, Annie was running upstairs.

That evening, all of us sat down to discuss all this Reconstruction stuff going on. Dad went on to say, "One of the things that must be done is each individual state has to amend their constitutions to abolish slavery forever, to pledge allegiance to the United States, and to vote for the 14th Amendment that permanently abolishes slavery in this country. Most of the states seem to be in agreement with what has been proposed, but the biggest problem is completely rejoining the Union. There's still too much hatred, and I feel that this country will never be whole again."

We've been home a couple of weeks now, and I fully see what Mom was talking about in that letter—and it's just as bad. The riots and the clashes are becoming more and more violent, and they have also become deadly.

Mine and Annie's Wedding

We've started planning our wedding—well, Annie and Emily have—and plan on it being at the house in a couple of weeks. I have to admit that I'm excited about spending the rest of my life with her and raising a family in peace. Annie keeps saying she wants to tell me something, but whenever I ask her, she just smiles and walks away. I know she's doing it on purpose because she knows it drives me insane.

I saw her outside on the porch looking like she'd been crying. I sat down beside her, and she looked at me and said four words that forever changed me: "I'm pregnant… with twins." I truly felt like I'd been hit with a cannonball in the chest. I was in complete shock. I stood up, helped her to her feet, and gave her a long kiss. I was going to be a dad. When we announced it to the family that evening, my mom passed out. Everyone was really happy for all involved. When Mom came to, she said, "A few months ago, I was praying and had a dream that night. I dreamed that both of you had found someone, and they both got pregnant, and one was carrying twins. I didn't believe much of it at first, but when I was told this tonight, that's why I passed out." Now everyone is sitting in silence, freaked out.

The wedding was a beautiful one. My beloved bride wore a traditional wedding dress that belonged to her mother, with daisies in her hair. She wanted to wear the dress in honor of her mother, and I told her that it was the greatest gift she could give her mom. As with Patrick and Emily, Annie wanted us to write our own vows.

Annie: "James, my beloved and forever husband, I love you more than life itself, and it is greater than all the stars in Heaven. When I first laid my eyes on you those years ago, I knew then that I would be your wife—even before I met you. I promise to honor, cherish, and obey as long as I live. I love you, James."

James: "I'm not as good at writing as she is, so I'll just say it. Annie, I love you with everything that I am. You kept me alive more than you will ever know. When I was in those prisoner-of-war camps, and on the long journey home, and especially on the battlefield, your love shielded me from death—and I will shield you too. I promise to honor, cherish, and obey as long as I live. I love you, Annie."

Delivery Time

Over the next few weeks and months, Patrick and I stayed away from the violence and issues that were happening. We both agreed that we had seen way too much violence and bloodshed to last ten lifetimes. We focused all our time on keeping our wives as comfortable as possible until delivery time.

In mid-September, Emily delivered a very healthy baby boy, and they named him Patrick Eugene Calloway, after both the daddies. A few weeks later, in early October, my precious Annie delivered twins—one of each. We named the girl Abigail Rose Calloway; that was Annie's idea. She wanted to do that in honor of Abigail's bravery and courage so her memory would live on. The boy was named Tyler Stephen Calloway. I was quite curious as to why "Stephen," and she said, "That was the place I said 'I do' to you, even before you knew I even existed."

In Summary

Going into writing this novel, I had no idea of the task at hand. I've always enjoyed writing, and back in school, I won awards for it—in horror. The completely ironic part is that I don't like horror movies. Most of my writings have been a few pages of absolutely random thoughts that somehow seem to fit together and make sense on paper.

So, when I came up with the idea to sit down and write another story, the thought of a novel wasn't even on the radar. After writing *The* Battle of Flintlock Valley, I let a friend read it, and he said one sentence that turned this from a story into a novel: "The characters aren't developed enough." Thanks, Greg.

Even a year ago, I would've never dreamed about writing this. Life can be full of surprises, and I think that's one thing that makes life fun—we never know what lies around the next corner. Oftentimes in life, we limit ourselves out of the fear of failure or lack of confidence. So, at the end of the day, I say just jump—because you never know where you will land.

Acknowledgements

This, or any other of my stories, would not be possible without my Lord and Savior, Jesus Christ, who blessed me with the ability to write. There are a few others I want to specifically acknowledge for their help:

- Stephanie, for listening—or at least I hope—listening to my ramblings about this and other things.

- To my dear friend Johnathon for pushing me with the idea to write. You will always be my brother.

- Diane, thank you from the bottom of my heart—you have been a great help.

- Emma from the library, whom I'm sure I got on her nerves with my sometimes never-ending questions.

Greg and Timmy, thank you for your honest (and sometimes painfully true) assessments of this.

Dedication

This book is humbly dedicated to my mom and dad. Even though they are now gone, their strength and love will live with me for life. I also want to dedicate it to my three children, whom I love dearly.